Annie wanted anonymity…

…Lydia wanted the spotlight.

They both found love.…

This month: *Christmas Angel for the Billionaire*

Lady Napier has been in the
media spotlight most of her life, especially since
taking over her parents' charity work. Now
Annie wants a break from being the "nation's angel,"
so she goes undercover…

Next month: *Her Desert Dream*

…and her look-alike, girl-next-door Lydia Young,
takes Annie's place for the week! Lydia thinks that
a holiday in the desert kingdom of Ramal Hamrah
with a gorgeous sheikh doesn't sound like much of
a chore but she's in for a surprise!

LIZ FIELDING

Christmas Angel
for the Billionaire

Christmas
Treats

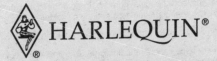

HARLEQUIN®

TORONTO • NEW YORK • LONDON
AMSTERDAM • PARIS • SYDNEY • HAMBURG
STOCKHOLM • ATHENS • TOKYO • MILAN • MADRID
PRAGUE • WARSAW • BUDAPEST • AUCKLAND

Recycling programs for this product may not exist in your area.

ISBN-13: 978-0-373-18477-4

CHRISTMAS ANGEL FOR THE BILLIONAIRE

First North American Publication 2009.

This edition published by arrangement with Harlequin Books S.A.

® and TM are trademarks of the publisher. Trademarks indicated with ® are registered in the United States Patent and Trademark Office, the Canadian Trade Marks Office and in other countries.

www.eHarlequin.com

Printed in U.S.A.

Liz Fielding was born with itchy feet. She made it to Zambia before her twenty-first birthday and, gathering her own special hero and a couple of children on the way, lived in Botswana, Kenya and Bahrain—with pauses for sightseeing pretty much everywhere in between. She finally came to a full stop in a tiny Welsh village cradled by misty hills, and these days she mostly leaves her pen to do the traveling. When she's not sorting out the lives and loves of her characters she potters in the garden, reads her favourite authors and spends a lot of time wondering "What if…?" For news of upcoming books—and to sign up for her occasional newsletter—visit Liz's Web site at www.lizfielding.com.

This season Harlequin® Romance brings you

For an extra-special treat this Christmas
don't look under the Christmas tree or in
your stocking—pick up one of your favorite
Harlequin Romance novels, curl up and relax!

From presents to proposals, mistletoe to marriage,
we promise to deliver seasonal warmth, wonder
and of course the unbeatable rush of romance!

*And look out for Christmas surprises
this month in Harlequin Romance!*

PROLOGUE

Daily Chronicle, 19th December, 1988

MARQUESS AND WIFE SLAIN ON CHARITY MISSION

The Marquess and Marchioness of St Ives, whose fairy-tale romance captured the hearts of the nation, were slain yesterday by rebels who opened fire on their vehicle as they approached a refugee camp in the war-torn region of Mishona. Their driver and a local woman who worked for the medical charity Susie's Friends *also died in the attack.*

HM the Queen sent a message of sympathy to the Duke of Oldfield, the widowed father of the Marquess, and to the slaughtered couple's six-year-old daughter, Lady Roseanne Napier.

The Marchioness of St Ives, Lady Susanne Napier, who overcame early hardships to train as a doctor, founded the international emergency charity with her husband shortly after their marriage.

Daily Chronicle, 24th December, 1988

WE MUST ALL BE HER FAMILY NOW...

Six-year-old Lady Roseanne Napier held her grand-father's hand as the remains of her slain mother and father were laid to rest in the family vault yesterday afternoon. In his oration, praising their high ideals, the grieving Duke said, 'We must all be her family now...'

Daily Chronicle, 18th December, 1998

A PERFECT ANGEL...

Today, on the tenth anniversary of the slaying of her parents while helping to co-ordinate relief in war-ravished Mishona, Lady Rose Napier opened Susanne House, a children's hospice named to honour her mother. After unveiling a plaque, Lady Rose met the brave children who are being cared for at Susanne House and talked to their parents. 'She was so caring, so thoughtful for someone so young,' one of the nurses said. 'A perfect angel. Her mother would have been so proud of her.'

Her mother isn't here to tell her that, so we are saying it for her.

We are all proud of you, Lady Rose.

CHAPTER ONE

ANNIE smothered a yawn. The room was hot, the lingering scent of food nauseating and all she wanted to do was lay her head on the table in front of her, close her eyes and switch off.

If only.

There was a visit to a hospital, then three hours of Wagner at a charity gala to endure before she could even think about sleep. And even then, no matter how tired she was, thinking about it was as close as she would get.

She'd tried it all. Soothing baths, a lavender pillow, every kind of relaxation technique without success. But calming her mind wasn't the problem.

It wasn't the fact that it was swirling with all the things she needed to remember that was keeping her awake. She had an efficient personal assistant to take care of every single detail of her life and ensure that she was in the right place at the right time. A speech writer to put carefully chosen words into her mouth when she got there. A style consultant whose job it was to ensure that whenever she appeared in public she made the front page.

That *was* the problem.

There was absolutely nothing in her mind to swirl around. It was empty. Like her life.

In just under a minute she was going to have to stand up and talk to these amazing people who had put themselves on the line to alleviate suffering in the world.

They had come to see her, listen to her inspire them to even greater efforts. And her presence ensured that the press was here too, which meant that the work they did would be noticed, reported.

Maybe.

Her hat, a rich green velvet and feather folly perched at a saucy angle over her right eye would probably garner more column inches than the charity she was here to support.

She was doing more for magazine and newspaper circulation than she was for the medical teams, the search units, pilots, drivers, communications people who dropped everything at a moment's notice, risking their lives to help victims of war, famine, disaster—a point she'd made to her grandfather more than once.

A pragmatist, he had dismissed her concerns, reminding her that it was a symbiotic relationship and everyone would benefit from her appearance, including the British fashion industry.

It didn't help that he was right.

She wanted to do more, *be* more than a cover girl, a fashion icon. Her parents had been out there, on the front line, picking up the pieces of ruined lives and she had planned to follow in their footsteps.

She stopped the thought. Publicity was the only gift she had and she had better do it right but, as she took her place at the lectern and a wave of applause hit her, a long silent scream invaded the emptiness inside her head.

Noooooo…

'Friends…' she began when the noise subsided. She paused, looked around her, found faces in the audience she recognised, people her parents had known. Took a breath, dug deep, smiled. 'I hope I've earned the right to call you that…'

She had been just eighteen years old when, at her grandfather's urging, she'd accepted an invitation to become patron of Susie's Friends. A small consolation for the loss of her dream of following her mother into medicine.

All that had ended when, at the age of sixteen, a photograph of her holding the hand of a dying child had turned her, overnight, from a sheltered, protected teen into an iconic image and her grandfather had laid out the bald facts for her.

How impossible it was. How her fellow students, patients even, would be harassed, bribed by the press for gossip about her because she was now public property. Then he'd consoled her with the fact that this way she could do so much more for the causes her mother had espoused.

Ten years on, more than fifty charities had claimed her as a patron. How many smiles, hand-shakes? Charity galas, first nights?

How many children's hands had she held, how many babies had she cradled?

None of them her own.

She had seen herself described as the 'most loved woman in Britain', but living in an isolation bubble, sheltered, protected from suffering the same fate as her parents, it was a love that never came close enough to touch.

But the media was a hungry beast that had to be fed and it was, apparently, time to move the story on. Time for a husband and children to round out the image. And, being her grandfather, he wasn't prepared to leave anything that important to chance.

Or to her.

Heaven forbid there should be anything as messy as her own father's passionate romance with a totally unsuitable woman, one whose ideals had ended up getting them both killed.

Instead, he'd found the perfect candidate in Rupert Devenish, Viscount Earley, easing him into her life so subtly that she'd barely noticed. Titled, rich and almost too good-looking to be true, he was so eligible that if she'd gone to the 'ideal husband' store and picked him off the shelf he couldn't be more perfect.

So perfect, in fact, that unless she was extremely careful, six months from now she'd find herself with a ring on her finger and in a year she'd be on every front page, every magazine cover, wearing the 'fairy-tale' dress. The very thought of it weighed like a lump of lead somewhere in the region of her heart. Trapped, with nowhere to turn, she felt as if the glittering chandeliers were slowly descending to crush her.

She dug her nails into her palm to concentrate her mind, took a sip of water, looked around at all the familiar faces and, ignoring the carefully worded speech that had been written for her, she talked to them about her parents, about ideals, about sacrifice, her words coming straight from the heart.

An hour later it was over and she turned to the hotel manager as he escorted her to the door. 'Another wonderful lunch, Mr Gordon. How is your little girl?'

'Much improved, thank you, Lady Rose. She was so thrilled with the books you sent her.'

'She wrote me the sweetest note.' She glanced at the single blush-pink rose she was holding.

She yearned to be offered, just once, something outrageous in purple or orange, but this variety of rose had been named for her and part of the proceeds of every sale went to Susanne House. To have offered her anything else would have been unthinkable.

'Will you give her this from me?' she said, offering him the rose.

'Madam,' he said, pink with pleasure as he took it and Annie felt a sudden urge to hug the man. Instead, she let her hand rest briefly on his arm before she turned to join Rupert, who was already at the door, impatient to be away.

Turned and came face to face with herself.

Or at least a very close facsimile.

A look in one of the mirrors that lined the walls would have shown two tall, slender young women, each with pale gold hair worn up in the same elegant twist, each with harebell-blue eyes.

Annie had been aware of her double's existence for years. Had seen photographs in magazines and newspapers, courtesy of the cuttings agency that supplied clippings of any print article that contained her name. She'd assumed that the amazing likeness had been aided by photographic manipulation but it wasn't so. It was almost like looking in the mirror.

For a moment they both froze. Annie, more experienced in dealing with the awkward moment, putting people at their ease, was the first to move.

'I know the face,' she said, feeling for the woman—it wasn't often a professional 'lookalike' came face to face with the real thing. With a smile, she added, 'But I'm afraid the name escapes me.'

Her double, doing a remarkable job of holding her poise under the circumstances, said, 'Lydia, madam.

Lydia Young.' But, as she took her hand, Annie felt it shaking. 'I'm s-so sorry. I promise this wasn't planned. I had no idea you'd be here.'

'Please, it's not a problem.' Then, intrigued, 'Do you—or do I mean I?—have an engagement here?'

'Had. A product launch.' Lydia gave an awkward little shrug as she coloured up. 'A new variety of tea.'

'I do hope it's good,' Annie replied, 'if I'm endorsing it.'

'Well, it's expensive,' Lydia said, relaxing sufficiently to smile back. Then, 'I'll just go and sit down behind that pillar for ten minutes, shall I? While I'm sure the photographers out there would enjoy it if we left together, my clients didn't pay me anywhere near enough to give them that kind of publicity.'

'It would rather spoil the illusion if we were seen together,' Annie agreed. About to walk on, something stopped her. 'As a matter of interest, Lydia, how much do you charge for being me?' she asked. 'Just in case I ever decide to take a day off.'

'No charge for you, Lady Rose,' she replied, handing her the rose that she was, inevitably, carrying as she sank into a very brief curtsey. 'Just give me a call. Any time.'

For a moment they looked at one another, then Annie sniffed the rose and said, 'They don't have much character, do they? No scent, no thorns...'

'Well, it's November. I imagine they've been forced under glass.'

Something they had in common, Annie thought.

She didn't have much character either, just a carefully manufactured image as the nation's 'angel', 'sweetheart'.

Rupert, already through the door, looked back to see what was keeping her and, apparently confident enough to display a little impatience, said, 'Rose, we're running late…'

They both glanced in his direction, then Lydia looked at her and lifted a brow in a 'dump the jerk' look that exactly mirrored her own thoughts.

'I don't suppose you fancy three hours of Wagner this evening?' she asked but, even before Lydia could reply, she shook her head. 'Just kidding. I wouldn't wish that on you.'

'I meant what I said.' And Lydia, taking a card from the small clutch bag she was carrying, offered it to her. 'Call me. Any time.'

Three weeks later, as speculation in the press that she was about to announce her engagement reached fever-pitch, Annie took out Lydia's card and dialled the number.

'Lydia Young…'

'Did you mean it?' she asked.

George Saxon, bare feet propped on the deck rail of his California beach house, laptop on his knees, gave up on the problem that had been eluding him for weeks and surfed idly through the headlines of the London newspapers.

His eye was caught by the picture of a couple leaving some gala. She was one of those tall patrician women, pale blonde hair swept up off her neck, her fabulously expensive gown cut low to reveal hollows in her shoulders even deeper than those in her cheeks.

But it wasn't her dress or the fact that she'd so obviously starved herself to get into it that had caught and held his attention. It was her eyes.

Her mouth was smiling for the camera, but her eyes, large, blue, seemed to be looking straight at him, sending him a silent appeal for help.

He clicked swiftly back to the program he'd been working on. Sometimes switching in and out of a problem cleared the blockage but this one was stubborn, which was why he'd left his Chicago office, lakeside apartment. Escaping the frantic pre-Christmas party atmosphere for the peace—and warmth—of the beach.

Behind him, inside the house, the phone began to ring. It would be his accountant, or his lawyer, or his office but success had insulated him from the need to jump when the phone rang and he left it for the machine to pick up. There was nothing, no one—

'George? It's your dad…'

But, then again, there were exceptions to every rule.

* * *

Tossing a holdall onto the back seat of the little red car that was Lydia's proudest possession, Annie settled herself behind the wheel and ran her hands over the steering wheel as if to reassure herself that it was real.

That she'd escaped...

Three hours ago, Lady Rose Napier had walked into a London hotel without her unshakeable escort—the annual Pink Ribbon Lunch was a ladies-only occasion. Two hours later, Lydia had walked out in her place. And ten minutes ago she'd left the same hotel completely unnoticed.

By now Lydia would be on board a private jet, heading for a week of total luxury at Bab el Sama, the holiday home of her friend Lucy al-Khatib.

Once there, all she had to do was put in an occasional appearance on the terrace or the beach for the paparazzi who, after the sudden rash of 'Wedding Bells?' headlines, would no doubt be sitting offshore in small boats, long-range cameras at the ready, hoping to catch her in flagrante in this private 'love-nest' with Rupert.

She hoped they'd packed seasick pills along with their sunscreen since they were going to have a very long wait.

And she grinned. She'd told her grandfather that she needed time on her own to consider her future. Not true. She wasn't going to waste one precious second of the time that Lydia—bless her heart—had given her thinking about Rupert Devenish.

She had just a week in which to be anonymous, to step outside the hothouse environment in which she'd lived since her parents had been killed. To touch reality as they had done. Be herself. Nothing planned, nothing organised. Just take life as it came.

She adjusted the rear-view mirror to check her appearance. She'd debated whether to go with a wig or colour her hair but, having tried a wig—it was amazing what you could buy on the Internet—and realising that living in it 24/7 was not for her, she'd decided to go for a temporary change of hair colour, darkening it a little with the temporary rinse Lydia had provided.

But that would have taken time and, instead, in an act of pure rebellion, of liberation, she'd hacked it short with a pair of nail scissors. When she'd stopped, the short, spiky result was so shocking that she'd been grateful for the woolly hat Lydia had provided to cover it.

She pulled it down over her ears, hoping that Lydia, forced to follow her style, would forgive her. Pushed the heavy-framed 'prop' spectacles up her nose. And grinned. The sense of freedom was giddying and, if she was honest, a little frightening. She'd never been completely on her own before and, shivering a little, she turned on the heater.

'Not frightening,' she said out loud as she eased

out of the parking bay and headed for the exit. 'Challenging.' And, reaching the barrier, she encountered her first challenge.

Lydia had left the ticket on the dashboard for her and she stuck it in the machine, expecting the barrier to lift. The machine spat it back out.

As she tried it the other way, with the same result, there was a series of impatient toots from the tailback building up behind her.

So much for invisibility.

She'd been on her own for not much more than an hour and already she was the centre of attention...

'What's your problem, lady?'

Annie froze but the 'Rose' never came and she finally looked up to find a car park attendant, a Santa Claus hat tugged down to his ears against the cold, glaring at her.

Apparently he'd used the word 'lady' not as a title, but as something barely short of an insult and, like his sour expression, it didn't quite match the 'ho, ho, ho' of the hat.

'Well?' he demanded.

'Oh. Um...' *Concentrate!* 'I put the ticket in, but nothing happened.'

'Have you paid?'

'Paid?' she asked. 'Where?'

He sighed. 'Can't you read? There's a notice ten feet high at the entrance.' Then, since she was still frowning, he said, very slowly, 'You have to pay before you leave. Over there.' She looked around, saw a machine, then, as the hooting became more insistent, 'In your own time,' he added sarcastically.

And *Bah! Humbug...* to you, she thought as she grabbed her bag from the car and sprinted to the nearest machine, read the instructions, fed in the ticket and then the amount indicated with shaking fingers.

She returned to the car, calling, 'Sorry, sorry...' to the people she'd held up before flinging herself back into the car and finally escaping.

Moments later, she was just one of thousands of drivers battling through traffic swollen by Christmas shoppers and visitors who'd come up to town to see the lights.

Anonymous, invisible, she removed the unnecessary spectacles, dropping them on the passenger seat, then headed west out of London.

She made good time but the pale blue winter sky was tinged with pink, the trees black against the horizon as she reached the junction for Maybridge. A pretty town with excellent shops, a popular riverside area, it was not too big, not too small. As good a place as any to begin her adventure and she headed for the ring road and the anonymous motel she'd found on the Internet.

Somewhere to spend the night and decide what she was going to do with her brief moment of freedom.

* * *

George Saxon's jaw was rigid as he kept his silence.

'No one else can do it,' his father insisted.

A nurse appeared, checked the drip. 'I need to make Mr Saxon comfortable,' she said. Then, with a pointed look at him, 'Why don't you take your mother home? She's been here all day.'

'No, I'll stay.' She took his father's hand, squeezed it. 'I'll be back in a little while.'

His father ignored her, instead grabbing his wrist as he made a move.

'Tell me you'll do it!'

'Don't fret,' his mother said soothingly. 'You can leave George to sort things out at the garage. He won't let you down.'

She looked pleadingly across the bed at him, silently imploring him to back her up.

'Of course he'll let me down,' his father said before he could speak. 'He never could stand getting his hands dirty.'

'Enough!' the nurse said and, not waiting for his mother, George walked from the room.

She caught up with him in the family room. 'I'm sorry—'

'Don't! Don't apologise for him.' Then, pouring her a cup of tea from one of the flasks on the trolley, 'You do realise that he's not going to be able to carry on like this?'

'Please, George...' she said.

Please, George...

Those two words had been the soundtrack to his childhood, his adolescence.

'I'll sort out what needs to be done,' he said. 'But maybe it's time for that little place by the sea?' he suggested, hoping to get her to see that there was an upside to this.

She shook her head. 'He'd be dead within a year.'

'He'll be dead anyway if he carries on.' Then, because he knew he was only distressing his mother, he said, 'Will you be okay here on your own? Have you had anything to eat?'

'I'll get myself something if I'm hungry,' she said, refusing to be fussed over. Then, her hand on his arm, 'I'm so grateful to you for coming home. Your dad won't tell you himself…' She gave an awkward little shrug. 'I don't have to tell you how stubborn he can be. But he's glad to see you.'

The traffic was building up to rush-hour level by the time Annie reached the far side of Maybridge. Unused to driving in heavy traffic, confused by the signs, she missed the exit for the motel, a fact she only realised when she passed it, seeing its lights blazing.

Letting slip a word she'd never used before, she took the next exit and then, rather than retracing her route using the ring road, she turned left, certain that it would lead her back to the motel. Fifteen minutes later, in an unlit country lane that had meandered off in totally the wrong direction, she admitted defeat and, as her headlights picked up the gateway to a field, she pulled over.

She found Reverse, swung the wheel and backed in. There was an unexpectedly sharp dip and the rear wheels left the tarmac with a hard bump, jolting the underside of the car.

Annie took a deep breath, told herself that it was nothing, then, having gathered herself, she turned the steering wheel in the right direction and applied a little pressure to the accelerator.

The only response was a horrible noise.

George sat for a moment looking up at the sign, George Saxon and Son, above the garage workshop. It was only when he climbed from the car that he noticed the light still burning, no doubt forgotten in the panic when his father had collapsed.

Using the keys his mother had given him, he unlocked the side door. Only two of the bays were occupied.

The nearest held the vintage Bentley that his father was in such a state about. Beautiful, arcane, it was in constant use as a wedding car and the brake linings needed replacing.

As he reached for the light switch he heard the familiar clang of a spanner hitting concrete, a muffled curse.

'Hello?'

There was no response and, walking around the Bentley, he discovered a pair of feet encased in expensive sports shoes, jiggling as if in time to music, sticking out from beneath the bonnet.

He didn't waste his breath trying to compete with whatever the owner of the feet was listening to, but instead he tapped one of them lightly with the toe of his shoe.

The movement stopped.

Then a pair of apparently endless, overall-clad legs slid from beneath the car, followed by a slender body. Finally a girl's face appeared.

'*Alexandra?*'

'*George?*' she replied, mocking his disbelief with pure sarcasm. 'Gran told me you were coming but I didn't actually believe her.'

He was tempted to ask her why not, but instead went for the big one.

'What are you doing here?' And, more to the point, why hadn't his mother warned him that his daughter was there when she'd given him her keys?

'Mum's away on honeymoon with husband number three,' she replied, as if that explained everything. 'Where else would I go?' Then, apparently realising that lying on her back she was at something of a disadvantage, she put her feet flat on the concrete and rose in one fluid, effortless movement that made him feel old.

'And these days everyone calls me Xandra.'

'Xandra,' he repeated without comment. She'd been named, without reference to him, after her maternal grandmother, a woman who'd wanted him put up against a wall and shot for despoiling her little princess. It was probably just as well that at the time he'd been too numb with shock to laugh.

Indicating his approval, however, would almost certainly cause her to change back. Nothing he did was ever right. He'd tried so hard, loved her so much, but it had always been a battle between them. And, much as he'd have liked to blame her mother for that, he knew it wasn't her fault. He simply had no idea how to be a dad. The kind that a little girl would smile at, run to.

'I have no interest in your mother's whereabouts,' he said. 'I want to know why you're here instead of at school?'

She lifted her shoulders in an insolent shrug. 'I've been suspended.'

'Suspended?'

'Indefinitely.' Then with a second, epic, I-really-couldn't-care-less shrug, 'Until after Christmas, anyway. Not that it matters. I wouldn't go back if they paid me.'

'Unlikely, I'd have said.'

'If you offered to build them a new science lab I bet they'd be keen enough.'

'In that case *I'd* be the one paying them to take

you back,' he pointed out. 'What has your mother done about it?'

'Nothing. I told you. She's lying on a beach somewhere. With her phone switched off.'

'You could have called me.'

'And what? You'd have dropped everything and rushed across the Atlantic to play daddy? Who knew you cared?'

He clenched his teeth. He was his father all over again. Incapable of forming a bond, making contact with this child who'd nearly destroyed his life. Who, from the moment she'd been grudgingly placed in his arms, had claimed his heart.

He would have done anything for her, died for her if need be. Anything but give up the dream he'd fought tooth and nail to achieve.

All the money in the world, the house his ex-wife had chosen, the expensive education—nothing he'd done had countered that perceived desertion.

'Let's pretend for a moment that I do,' he said, matter-of-factly. 'What did you do?'

'Nothing.' She coloured slightly. 'Nothing much.' He waited. 'I hot-wired the head's car and took it for a spin, that's all.'

Hot-wired...

Apparently taking his shocked silence as encouragement to continue, she said, 'Honestly. Who'd have thought the Warthog would have made such a fuss?'

'You're not old enough to drive!' Then, because she'd grown so fast, was almost a woman, 'Are you?'

She just raised her eyebrows, leaving him to work it out for himself. He was right. He'd been nineteen when she was born, which meant that his daughter wouldn't be seventeen until next May. It would be six months before she could even apply for a licence.

'You stole a car, drove it without a licence, without insurance?' He somehow managed to keep his voice neutral. 'That's your idea of "nothing much"?'

He didn't bother asking who'd taught her to drive. That would be the same person who'd given him an old banger and let him loose in the field out back as soon as his feet touched the pedals. Driving was in the Saxon blood, according to his father, and engine oil ran through their veins.

But, since she'd hot-wired Mrs Warburton's car, clearly driving wasn't all her grandfather had taught her.

'What were you doing under the Bentley?' he demanded as a chill that had nothing to do with the temperature ran through him.

'Just checking it out. It needs new brake linings…' The phone began to ring. With the slightest of shrugs, she leaned around him, unhooked it from the wall and said, 'George Saxon and Granddaughter…'

What?

'Where are you?' she asked, reaching for a pen. 'Are you on your own…? Okay, stay with the car—'

George Saxon and Granddaughter...

Shock slowed him down and as he moved to wrest the phone from her she leaned back out of his reach.

'—we'll be with you in ten minutes.' She replaced the receiver. 'A lone woman broken down on the Longbourne Road,' she said. 'I told her we'll pick her up.'

'I heard what you said. Just how do you propose to do that?' he demanded furiously.

'Get in the tow-truck,' she suggested, 'drive down the road...'

'There's no one here to deal with a breakdown.'

'You're here. *I'm* here. Granddad says I'm as good as you were with an engine.'

If she thought that would make him feel better, she would have to think again.

'Call her back,' he said, pulling down the local directory. 'Tell her we'll find someone else to help her.'

'I didn't take her number.'

'It doesn't matter. She won't care who turns up so long as someone does,' he said, punching in the number of another garage. It had rung just twice when he heard the clunk as a truck door was slammed shut. On the third ring he heard it start.

He turned around as a voice in his ear said, 'Longbourne Motors. How can I...'

The personnel door was wide open and, as he

watched, the headlights of the pick-up truck pierced the dark.

'Sorry,' he said, dropping the phone and racing after his daughter, wrenching open the cab door as it began to move. 'Turn it off!'

She began to move as he reached for the keys.

'Alexandra! Don't you dare!' He hung onto the door, walking quickly alongside the truck as she moved across the forecourt.

'It's Granddad's business,' she said, speeding up a little, forcing him to run or let go. He ran. 'I'm not going to let you shut it down.' Then, having made her point, she eased off the accelerator until the truck rolled to a halt before turning to challenge him. 'I love cars, engines. I'm going to run this place, be a rally driver—'

'What?'

'Granddad's going to sponsor me.'

'You're sixteen,' he said, not sure whether he was more horrified that she wanted to race cars or fix them. 'You don't know what you want.'

Even as he said the words, he heard his father's voice. *'You're thirteen, boy. Your head is full of nonsense. You don't know what you want…'*

He'd gone on saying it to him even when he was filling in forms, applying for university places, knowing that he'd get no financial backing, that he'd have to support himself every step of the way.

Even when his 'nonsense' was being installed in

every new engine manufactured throughout the world, his father had still been telling him he was wrong…

'Move over,' he said.

Xandra clung stubbornly to the steering wheel. 'What are you going to do?'

'Since you've already kept a lone woman waiting in a dark country lane for five minutes longer than necessary, I haven't got much choice. I'm going to let you pick her up.'

'Me?'

'You. But you've already committed enough motoring offences for one week, so I'll drive the truck.'

CHAPTER TWO

ANNIE saw the tow-truck, yellow light flashing on the roof of the cab, looming out of the dark, and sighed with relief as it pulled up just ahead of her broken-down car.

After a lorry, driving much too fast along the narrow country lane, had missed the front of the car by inches, she'd scrambled out and was standing with her back pressed against the gate, shivering with the cold.

The driver jumped down and swung a powerful torch over and around the car, and she threw up an arm to shield her eyes from the light as he found her.

'George Saxon,' her knight errant said, lowering the torch a little. 'Are you okay?' he asked.

'Y-y-yes,' she managed through chattering teeth. She couldn't see his face behind the light but his voice had a touch of impatience that wasn't exactly what she'd hoped for. 'No thanks to a lorry driver who nearly took the front off the car.'

'You should have switched on the hazard warning

lights,' he said unsympathetically. 'Those sidelights are useless.'

'If he'd been driving within the speed limit, he'd have seen me,' she replied, less than pleased at the suggestion that it was her own fault that she'd nearly been killed.

'There is no speed limit on this road other than the national limit. That's seventy miles an hour,' he added, in case she didn't know.

'I saw the signs. Foolishly, perhaps, I assumed that it was the upper limit, not an instruction,' she snapped right back.

'True,' he agreed, 'but just because other people behave stupidly it doesn't mean you have to join in.'

First the car park attendant and now the garage mechanic. Irritable men talking to her as if she had dimwit tattooed across her forehead was getting tiresome.

Although, considering she could be relaxing in the warmth and comfort of Bab el Sama instead of freezing her socks off in an English country lane in December, they might just have a point.

'So,' he asked, gesturing at the car with the torch, 'what's the problem?'

'I thought it was your job to tell me that,' she replied, deciding she'd taken enough male insolence for one day.

'Okaaay…'

Back-lit by the bright yellow hazard light swinging around on top of the tow-truck, she couldn't make out more than the bulk of him but she had a strong sense of a man hanging onto his temper by a thread.

'Let's start with the basics,' he said, making an effort. 'Have you run out of petrol?'

'What kind of fool do you take me for?'

'That's what I'm trying to establish,' he replied with all the long-suffering patience of a man faced with every conceivable kind of a fool. Then, with a touch more grace, 'Maybe you should just tell me what happened and we'll take it from there.'

That was close enough to a truce to bring her from the safety of the gate and through teeth that were chattering with the cold—or maybe delayed shock, that lorry had been very close—she said, 'I t-took the wrong road and t-tried to—'

'To' turned into a yelp as she caught her foot in a rut and was flung forward, hands outstretched, as she grabbed for anything to save herself. What she got was soft brushed leather and George Saxon, who didn't budge as she cannoned into him but, steady as a rock, caught her, then held her as she struggled to catch her breath.

'Are you okay?' he asked after a moment.

With her cheek, her nose and her hands pressed against his chest, she was in no position to answer.

But with his breath warm against her skin, his

hands holding her safe, there wasn't a great deal wrong that she could think of.

Except, of course, all of the above.

She couldn't remember ever being quite this close to a man she didn't know, so what she was feeling—and whether 'okay' covered it—she couldn't begin to say. She was still trying to formulate some kind of response when he moved back slightly, presumably so that he could check for himself.

'I think so,' she said quickly, getting a grip on her wits. She even managed to ease back a little herself, although she didn't actually let go until she'd put a little weight on her ankle to test it.

There didn't appear to be any damage but she decided not to rush it.

'I'm in better shape than the car, anyway.'

He continued to look at her, not with the deferential respect she was used to, but in a way that made her feel exposed, vulnerable and, belatedly, she let go of his jacket, straightened the spectacles that had slipped sideways.

'It was d-dark,' she stuttered—*stuttered?* 'And when I backed into the gate there was a bit more of a d-drop than I expected.' Then, realising how feeble that sounded, 'Quite a lot more of a drop, actually. This field entrance is very badly maintained,' she added, doing her best to distance herself from the scent of leather warmed by a man's body. From the feel of his chest beneath it, his solid shoulders. The touch of strong hands.

And in the process managed to sound like a rather pompous and disapproving dowager duchess.

'Good enough for a tractor,' he replied, dropping those capable hands and taking a step back. Leaving a cold space between them. 'The farmer isn't in the business of providing turning places for women who can't read a map.'

'I…' On the point of saying that she hadn't looked at a map, she thought better of it. He already thought she was a fool and there was nothing to be gained from confirming his first impression. 'No. Well…' She'd have taken a step back herself if she hadn't been afraid her foot would find another rut and this time do some real damage. 'I banged the underside of the car on something as I went down. When I tried to drive away it made a terrible noise and…' She shrugged.

'And what?' he persisted.

'And nothing,' she snapped. Good grief, did he want it spelling out in words of one syllable? 'It wasn't going anywhere.' Then, rubbing her hands over her sleeves, 'Can you fix it?'

'Not here.'

'Oh.'

'Come on,' he said and, apparently taking heed of her comments about the state of the ground, he took her arm and supported her back onto the safety of the tarmac before opening the rear door of the truck's cab. 'You'd better get out of harm's way while we load her up.'

As the courtesy light came on, bathing them both in light, Annie saw more of him. The brushed leather bomber jacket topping long legs clad not, as she'd expected, in overalls, but a pair of well-cut light-coloured trousers. And, instead of work boots, he was wearing expensive-looking loafers. Clearly, George Saxon hadn't had the slightest intention of doing anything at the side of the road.

Her face must have betrayed exactly what she was thinking because he waved his torch over a tall but slight figure in dark overalls who was already attaching a line to her car.

'She's the mechanic,' he said with a sardonic edge to his voice. His face, all dark shadows as the powerful overhead light swung in the darkness, matched his tone perfectly. 'I'm just along for the ride.'

She? Annie thought as, looking behind her, he called out, 'How are you doing back there?'

'Two minutes…'

The voice was indeed that of a girl. Young and more than a little breathless and Annie, glancing back as she reached for the grab rail to haul herself up into the cab, could see that she was struggling.

'I think she could do with some help,' she said.

George regarded this tiresome female who'd been wished on him by his daughter with irritation.

'I'm just the driver,' he said. Then, offering her the torch, 'But don't let me stop you from pitching in and giving her a hand.'

'It's okay,' Xandra called before she could take it from him. 'I've got it.'

He shrugged. 'It seems you were worrying about nothing.'

'Are you sure?' she asked, calling back to Xandra while never taking her eyes off him. It was a look that reminded him of Miss Henderson, a teacher who had been able to quell a class of unruly kids with a glance. Maybe it was the woolly hat and horn-rimmed glasses.

Although he had to admit that Miss Henderson had lacked the fine bone structure and, all chalk and old books, had never smelt anywhere near as good.

'I'm done,' Xandra called.

'Happy?' he enquired.

The woman held the look for one long moment before she gave him a cool nod and climbed up into the cab, leaving him to close the door behind her as if she were royalty.

'Your servant, ma'am,' he muttered as he went back to see how Xandra was doing.

'Why on earth did you say that to her?' she hissed as he checked the coupling.

He wasn't entirely sure. Other than the fact that Miss Henderson was the only woman he'd ever known who could cut his cocky ten-year-old self down to size with a glance.

'Let's go,' he said, pretending he hadn't heard.

Back in the cab, he started the engine and began to winch the car up onto the trailer but, when he glanced up to check the road, his passenger's eyes, huge behind the lenses, seemed to fill the rear-view mirror.

'Can we drop you somewhere?' he asked as Xandra climbed in beside him. Eager to be rid of her so that he could drop the car off at Longbourne Motors.

That took the starch right out of her look.

'What? No… I can't go on without my car…'

'It's not going anywhere tonight. You don't live locally?' he asked.

'No. I'm… I'm on holiday. Touring.'

'On your own? In December?'

'Is there something wrong with that?'

A whole lot, in his opinion, but it was none of his business. 'Whatever turns you on,' he said, 'although Maybridge in winter wouldn't be my idea of a good time.'

'Lots of people come for the Christmas market,' Xandra said. 'It's this weekend. I'm going.'

All this and Christmas too. How much worse could it get? he thought before turning to Xandra and saying, 'You aren't going anywhere. You're grounded.' Then, without looking in the mirror, he said, 'Where are you staying tonight?'

'I'm not booked in anywhere. I was heading for the motel on the ring road.'

'We'd have to go all the way to the motorway roundabout to get there from here,' Xandra said before he could say a word, no doubt guessing his intention of dropping the car off at Longbourne Motors. 'Much easier to run the lady back to the motel through the village once we have a better idea of how long it will take to fix her car.'

She didn't wait for an answer, instead turning to introduce herself to their passenger. 'I'm sorry, I'm Xandra Saxon,' she said, but she was safe enough. This wasn't an argument he planned on having in front of a stranger.

Annie relaxed a little as George Saxon took his eyes off her and smiled at the girl beside him, who was turning into something of an ally.

'Hello, Xandra. I'm R-Ro…'

The word began to roll off her tongue before she remembered that she wasn't Rose Napier.

'Ro-o-owland,' she stuttered out, grabbing for the first name that came into her head. Nanny Rowland… 'Annie Rowland,' she said, more confidently.

Lydia had suggested she borrow her name but she'd decided that it would be safer to stick with something familiar. Annie had been her mother's pet name for her but, since her grandfather disapproved of it, no one other than members of the household staff who'd known her since her mother was alive had ever used it. In the stress of the moment, though, the practised response had gone clean out of her head and she'd slipped into her standard introduction.

'Ro-o-owland?' George Saxon, repeating the name with every nuance of hesitation, looked up at the rear-view mirror and held her gaze.

'Annie will do just fine,' she said, then, realising that man and girl had the same name, she turned to Xandra. 'You're related?'

'Not so's you'd notice,' she replied in that throwaway, couldn't-care-less manner that the young used when something was truly, desperately important. 'My mother has made a career of getting married. George was the first in line, with a shotgun to his back if the date on my birth certificate is anything—'

'Buckle up, Xandra,' he said, cutting her off.

He was her father? But she wasn't, it would appear, daddy's little girl if the tension between them was anything to judge by.

But what did she know about the relationship between father and daughter? All she remembered was the joy of her father's presence, feeling safe in his arms. If he'd lived would she have been a difficult teen?

The one thing she wouldn't have been was isolated, wrapped in cotton wool by a grandfather afraid for her safety. She'd have gone to school, mixed with girls—and boys—her own age. Would have fallen in and out of love without the eyes of the entire country on her. Would never have stepped into the spotlight only to discover, too late, that she was unable to escape its glare.

'Are you warm enough back there?' George Saxon asked.

'Yes. Thank you.'

The heater was efficient and despite his lack of charm, he hadn't fumbled when she'd fallen into his arms. On the contrary. He'd been a rock and she felt safe enough in the back of his truck. A lot safer than she'd felt in his arms. But of course this was her natural place in the world. Sitting in the back with some man up front in the driving seat. In control.

Everything she'd hoped to escape from, she reminded herself, her gaze fixed on the man who was in control at the moment. Or at least the back of his head.

Over the years she had become something of a connoisseur of the back of the male head. The masculine neck. All those chauffeurs, bodyguards…

George Saxon's neck would stand comparison with the best, she decided. Strong, straight with thick dark hair expertly cut to exactly the right length. His shoulders, encased in the soft tan leather of his jacket, would take some beating too. It was a pity his manners didn't match them.

Or was she missing the point?

Rupert's perfect manners made her teeth ache to

say or do something utterly outrageous just to get a reaction, but George Saxon's hands, like his eyes, had been anything but polite.

They'd been assured, confident, brazen even. She could still feel the imprint of his thumbs against her breasts where his hands had gripped her as she'd fallen; none of that Dresden shepherdess nonsense for him. And his insolence as he'd offered her the torch had sent an elemental shiver of awareness running up her spine that had precious little to do with the cold that had seeped deep into her bones.

He might not be a gentleman, but he was real—dangerously so—and, whatever else he made her feel, it certainly wasn't desperation.

Annie didn't have time to dwell on what exactly he did make her feel before he swung the truck off the road and turned onto the forecourt of a large garage with a sign across the workshop that read, George Saxon and Son.

Faded and peeling, neglected, it didn't match the man, she thought as he backed up to one of the bays. He might be a little short on charm but he had an animal vitality that sent a charge of awareness running through her.

Xandra jumped down and opened the doors and then, once he'd backed her car in, she uncoupled it, he said, 'There's a customer waiting room at the far end. You'll find a machine for drinks.' Dismissed, she climbed down from the truck and walked away. 'Annie!'

She stopped. It was, she discovered, easy to be charming when everyone treated you with respect but she had to take a deep breath before she turned, very carefully, to face him.

'Mr Saxon?' she responded politely.

'Shut the damn door!'

She blinked.

No one had ever raised their voice to her. Spoken to her in that way.

'In your own time,' he said when she didn't move.

Used to having doors opened for her, stepping out of a car without so much as a backward glance, she hadn't even thought about it.

She wanted to be ordinary, she reminded herself. To be treated like an ordinary woman. Clearly, it was going to be an education.

She walked back, closed the door, but if she'd expected the courtesy of a thank you she would have been disappointed.

Always a fast learner, she hadn't held her breath.

'Take no notice of George,' Xandra said as he drove away to park the truck. 'He doesn't want to be here so he's taking it out on you.'

'Doesn't…? Why not? Isn't he the "and Son"?'

She laughed, but not with any real mirth. 'Wrong generation. The "and Son" above the garage is my granddad but he's in hospital. A heart attack.'

'I'm sorry to hear that. How is he?'

'Not well enough to run the garage until I can take over,' she said. Then, blinking back something that looked very much like a tear, she shrugged, lifted her head. 'Sorry. Family business.' She flicked a switch that activated the hoist. 'I'll take a look at your car.'

Annie, confused by the tensions, wishing she could do something too, but realising that she'd been dismissed—and that was new, as well—said, 'Your father mentioned a waiting room?'

'Oh, for goodness' sake. It'll be freezing in there and the drinks machine hasn't worked in ages.' Xandra fished a key out of her pocket. 'Go inside where it's warm,' she said, handing it to her. 'Make yourself at home. There's tea and coffee by the kettle, milk in the fridge.' Xandra watched the car as it rose slowly above them, then, realising that she hadn't moved, said, 'Don't worry. It won't take long to find the problem.'

'Are you quite sure?' she asked.

'I may be young but I know what I'm doing.'

'Yes…' Well, maybe. 'I meant about letting myself in.'

'Gran would invite you in herself if she were here,' she said as her father rejoined them.

In the bright strip light his face had lost the dangerous shadows, but it still had a raw quality. There was no softness to mitigate hard bone other than a full lower lip that oozed sensuality and only served to increase her sense of danger.

'You shouldn't be in here,' he said.

'I'm going…' She cleared her throat. 'Can I make something for either of you?' she offered.

He frowned.

She lifted her hand and dangled the door key. 'Tea? Coffee?'

For a moment she thought he was going to tell her to stay on her own side of the counter—maybe she was giving him the opportunity—but after a moment he shrugged and said, 'Coffee. If there is any.'

'Xandra?'

'Whatever,' she said, as she ducked beneath the hoist, clearly more interested in the car than in anything she had to say and Annie walked quickly across the yard, through a gate and up a well-lit path to the rear of a long, low stone-built house and let herself in through the back door.

The mud room was little more than a repository for boots and working clothes, a place to wash off the workplace dirt, but as she walked into the kitchen she was wrapped in the heat being belted out by an ancient solid fuel stove.

Now this was familiar, she thought, relaxing as she crossed to the sink, filled the kettle and set it on the hob to boil.

This room, so much more than a kitchen, was

typical of the farmhouses at King's Lacey, her grandfather's Warwickshire estate.

Her last memory of her father was being taken to visit the tenants before he'd gone away for the last time. She'd been given brightly coloured fizzy pop and mince pies while he'd talked to people he'd known since his boyhood, asking about their children and grandchildren, discussing the price of feedstuff, grain. She'd played with kittens, fed the chickens, been given fresh eggs to take home for her tea. Been a child.

She ran her hand over the large, scrubbed-top table, looked at the wide dresser, laden with crockery and piled up with paperwork. Blinked back the tear that caught her by surprise before turning to a couple of Morris armchairs, the leather seats scuffed and worn, the wooden arms rubbed with wear, one of them occupied by a large ginger cat.

A rack filled with copies of motoring magazines stood beside one, a bag stuffed with knitting beside the other. There was a dog basket by the Aga, but no sign of its owner.

She let the cat sniff her fingers before rubbing it behind the ear, starting up a deep purr. Comfortable, it was the complete opposite of the state-of-the-art kitchen in her London home. Caught in a nineteen-fifties time warp, the only concession to modernity here was a large refrigerator, its cream enamel surface chipped with age, and a small television set tucked away on a shelf unit built beside the chimney breast.

The old butler's sink, filled with dishes that were no doubt waiting for Xandra's attention—George Saxon didn't look the kind of man who was familiar with a dish mop—suggested that the age of the dishwasher had not yet reached the Saxon household.

She didn't have a lot of time to spare for basic household chores these days, but there had been a time, long ago, when she had been allowed to stand on a chair and wash dishes, help cook when she was making cakes and, even now, once in a while, when they were in the country, she escaped to the comfort of her childhood kitchen, although only at night, when the staff were gone.

She wasn't a child any more and her presence was an intrusion on their space.

Here, though, she was no one and she peeled off the woolly hat and fluffed up her short hair, enjoying the lightness of it. Then she hung her padded jacket on one of the pegs in the mud room before hunting out a pair of rubber gloves and pitching in.

Washing up was as ordinary as it got and she was grinning by the time she'd cleared the decks. It wasn't what she'd imagined she'd be doing this evening, but it certainly fulfilled the parameters of the adventure.

By the time she heard the back door open, the dishes were draining on the rack above the sink and she'd made a large pot of tea for herself and Xandra, and a cup of instant coffee for George.

'Oh…' Xandra came to an abrupt halt at the kitchen door as she saw the table on which she was laying out cups and saucers. 'I usually just bung a teabag in a mug,' she said. Then, glancing guiltily at the sink, her eyes widened further. 'You've done the washing-up…'

'Well, you did tell me to make myself at home,' Annie said, deadpan.

It took Xandra a moment but then she grinned. 'You're a brick. I *was* going to do it before Gran got home.'

A brick? No one had ever called her that before.

'Don't worry about it,' she replied, pouring tea while Xandra washed her hands at the sink. 'Your gran is at the hospital with your grandfather, I imagine?'

Before Xandra could answer, George Saxon followed her into the kitchen, bringing with him a metallic blast of cold air.

He came to an abrupt halt, staring at her for a moment. Or, rather, she thought, her hair, and she belatedly wished she'd kept her hat on, but it was too late for that.

'Has she told you?' he demanded, finally tearing his gaze away from what she knew must look an absolute fright.

'Told me what?' she asked him.

'That you've broken your crankshaft.'

'No,' she said, swiftly tiring of the novelty of his rudeness. A gentleman would have ignored the fact that she was having a seriously bad hair day rather than staring at the disaster in undisguised horror. 'I gave my ankle a bit of a jolt in that pothole but, unless things have changed since I studied anatomy, I don't believe that I have a crankshaft.'

Xandra snorted tea down her nose as she laughed, earning herself a quelling look from her father.

'You've broken the crankshaft that drives the wheels of your car,' he said heavily, quashing any thought she might have of joining in. 'It'll have to be replaced.'

'If I knew what a crankshaft was,' she replied, 'I suspect that I'd be worried. How long will it take?'

He shrugged. 'I'll have to ring around in the morning and see if there's anyone who can deal with it as an emergency.'

Annie heard what he said but even when she ran through it again it still made no sense.

'Why?' she asked finally.

He had the nerve to turn a pair of slate-grey eyes on her and regard her as if her wits had gone begging.

'I assume you want it repaired?'

'Of course I want it repaired. That's why I called you. You're a garage. You fix cars. So fix it.'

'I'm sorry but that's impossible.'

'You don't sound sorry.'

'He isn't. While Granddad's lying helpless in hospital he's going to shut down a garage that's been in the family for nearly a hundred years.'

'Are you?' she asked, keeping her gaze fixed firmly on him. 'That doesn't sound very sporting.'

He looked right back and she could see a pale fan of lines around his eyes that in anyone else she'd have thought were laughter lines.

'He flew all the way from California for that very purpose,' his daughter said when he didn't bother to answer.

'California?' Well, that certainly explained the lines around his eyes. Screwing them up against the sun rather than an excess of good humour. 'How interesting. What do you do in California, Mr Saxon?'

Her life consisted of asking polite questions, drawing people out of their shell, showing an interest. She had responded with her 'Lady Rose' voice and she'd have liked to pretend that this was merely habit rather than genuine interest, but that would be a big fat fib. There was something about George Saxon that aroused a lot more than polite interest in her maidenly breast.

His raised eyebrow suggested that what he did in the US was none of her business and he was undoubtedly right, but his daughter was happy to fill the gap.

'According to my mother,' she said, 'George is a beach bum.'

At this point 'Lady Rose' would have smiled politely and moved on. Annie didn't have to do that.

'Is your mother right?' she asked.

'He doesn't go to work unless he feels like it. Lives on the beach. If it looks like a duck and walks like a duck…'

She was looking at George, talking to him, but the replies kept coming from his daughter, stage left, and Annie shook her head just once, lifted a hand to silence the girl, waiting for him to answer her question.

CHAPTER THREE

'I'M AFRAID it's your bad luck that my daughter answered your call,' George replied, not bothering to either confirm or deny it. 'If I'd got to the phone first I'd have told you to ring someone else.'

'I see. So why didn't you simply call another garage and arrange for them to pick me up?' Annie asked, genuinely puzzled.

'It would have taken too long and, since you were on your own...' He let it go.

She didn't.

'Oh, I *see*. You're a gentleman beach bum?'

'Don't count on it,' he replied.

No. She wouldn't do that, but he appeared to have a conscience and she could work with that.

She'd had years of experience in parting millionaires from their money in a good cause and this seemed like a very good moment to put what she'd learned to use on her own behalf.

'It's a pity your concern doesn't stretch as far as fixing my car.' Since his only response was to remove his jacket and hang it over the back of a chair, the clearest statement that he was going nowhere, she continued. 'So, George…' use his name, imply that they were friends '…having brought me here under false pretences, what do you suggest I do now?'

'I suggest you finish your tea, Annie…' and the way he emphasized her name suggested he knew exactly what game she was playing '…then I suggest you call a taxi.'

Well, that didn't go as well as she'd hoped.

'I thought the deal was that you were going to run me there,' she reminded him.

'It's been a long day. You'll find a directory by the phone. It's through there. In the hall,' he added, just in case she was labouring under the misapprehension that he would do it for her. Then, having glanced at the cup of instant coffee and the delicate china cups she'd laid out, he took a large mug—one that *she'd* just washed—from the rack over the sink and filled it with tea.

Annie had been raised to be a lady and her first reaction, even under these trying circumstances, was to apologise for being a nuisance.

There had been a moment, right after that lorry had borne down on her out of the dark and she'd thought her last moment had come, when the temptation to accept defeat had very nearly got the better of her.

Shivering with shock at her close brush with eternity as much as the cold, it would have been so easy to put in the call that would bring a chauffeur-driven limousine to pick her up, return her home with nothing but a very bad haircut and a lecture on irresponsibility from her grandfather to show for her adventure.

But she'd wanted reality and that meant dealing with the rough as well as the smooth. Breaking down on a dark country road was no fun, but Lydia wouldn't have been able to walk away, leave someone else to pick up the pieces. She'd have to deal with the mechanic who'd responded to her call, no matter how unwillingly. How lacking in the ethos of customer service.

Lydia, she was absolutely certain, wouldn't apologise to him for expecting him to do his job, but demand he got on with it.

She could do no less.

'I'm sorry,' she began, but she wasn't apologising for being a nuisance. Far from it. Instead, she picked up her tea and polite as you please, went on. 'I'm afraid that is quite unacceptable. When you responded to my call you entered into a contract and I insist that you honour it.'

George Saxon paused in the act of spooning sugar into his tea and glanced up at her from beneath a lick of dark hair that had slid across his forehead.

'Is that right?' he asked.

He didn't sound particularly impressed.

'Under the terms of the Goods and Services Act,' she added, with the poise of a woman for whom addressing a room full of strangers was an everyday occurrence, 'nineteen eighty-three.' The Act was real enough, even if she'd made up the date. The trick was to look as if you knew what you were talking about and a date—even if it was the first one that came into her head—added veracity to even the most outrageous statement.

This time he did smile and deep creases bracketed his face, his mouth, fanned out around those slate eyes. Maybe not just the sun, then…

'You just made that up, Annie Rowland,' he said, calling her bluff.

She pushed up the spectacles that kept sliding down her nose and smiled right back.

'I'll just wait here while you go to the local library and check,' she said, lowering herself into the unoccupied Morris chair. 'Unless you have a copy?' Balancing the saucer in one hand, she used the other to pick up her tea and sip it. 'Although, since you're clearly unfamiliar with the legislation, I'm assuming that you don't.'

'The library is closed until tomorrow morning,' he pointed out.

'They don't have late-night opening? How inconvenient for you. Never mind, I can wait.' Then added, 'Or you could just save time and fix my car.'

George had known the minute Annie Ro-o-ow-land had blundered into him, falling into his arms as if she was made to fit, that he was in trouble. Then she'd looked at him through the rear-view mirror of the truck with those big blue eyes and he'd been certain of it. And here, in the light of his mother's kitchen, they had double the impact.

They were not just large, but were the mesmerizing colour of a bluebell wood in April, framed by long dark lashes and perfectly groomed brows that were totally at odds with that appalling haircut. At odds with those horrible spectacles which continually slipped down her nose as if they were too big for her face…

As he stared at her, the certainty that he'd seen her somewhere before tugging at his memory, she used one finger to push them back up and he knew without doubt that they were nothing more than a screen for her to hide behind.

Everything about her was wrong.

Her car, bottom of range even when new, was well past its best, her hair was a nightmare and her clothes were chain-store basics but her scent, so faint that he knew she'd sprayed it on warm skin hours ago, probably after her morning shower, was the real one-thousand-dollar-an-ounce deal.

And then there was her voice.

No one spoke like that unless they were born to it. Not even twenty-five thousand pounds a year at

Dower House could buy that true-blue aristocratic accent, a fact he knew to his cost.

He stirred his tea, took a sip, making her wait while he thought about his next move.

'I'll organise a rental for you while it's being fixed,' he offered finally. Experience had taught him that, where women were concerned, money was the easiest way to make a problem go away. But first he'd see how far being helpful would get him. 'If that would make things easier for you?'

She carefully replaced the delicate bone china cup on its saucer. 'I'm sorry, George. I'm afraid that's out of the question.'

It was like a chess game, he thought. Move and countermove. And everything about her—the voice, the poise—suggested that she was used to playing the Queen.

Tough. He wasn't about to be her pawn. He might be lumbered with Mike Jackson's Bentley—he couldn't offload a specialist job like that at short notice as his father well knew—but he wasn't about to take on something that any reasonably competent mechanic could handle.

Maybe if she took off her glasses…

'As a gesture of goodwill, recognising that you have been put to unnecessary inconvenience,' he said, catching himself—this was not the moment to allow himself to be distracted by a pair of blue eyes, pale flawless skin, scent that aroused an instant go-to-hell response. He didn't do 'instant'. It would have to be money. 'I would be prepared to pay any reasonable out-of-pocket expenses.'

Check.

He didn't care how much it cost to get her and her eyes out of the garage, out of his mother's kitchen, out of his hair. Just as long as she went.

'That's a most generous offer,' she replied. 'Unfortunately, I can't accept. The problem isn't money, you see, but my driving licence.'

'Oh?' Then, 'You do *have* a valid licence?'

If she was driving without one all bets were off. He could ground his daughter for her reckless behaviour—maybe—but Annie Rowland would be out of here faster than he could call the police.

But she wasn't in the least bit put out by his suggestion that she was breaking the law.

'I do have a driving licence,' she replied, cool as you like. 'And, in case you're wondering, it's as clean as the day it was issued. But I'm afraid I left it at home. In my other bag.' She shrugged. 'You know how it is.' Then, looking at him as if she'd only just noticed that he was a man, she smiled and said, 'Oh, no. I don't suppose you do. All a man has to do is pick up his wallet and he has everything he needs right there in his jacket pocket.'

He refused to indulge the little niggle that wanted to know whose wallet, what man…

'And where, exactly, is home?' he asked, trying

not to look at her hand and failing. She wasn't wearing a ring but that meant nothing.

'London.'

'London is a big place.'

'Yes,' she agreed. 'It is.' Then, without indulging his curiosity about which part of London, 'You must know that no one will rent me a car without it. My licence.'

Unfortunately, he did.

Checkmate.

'Oh, for goodness' sake!' Xandra, who'd been watching this exchange with growing impatience, said, 'If you won't fix Annie's car, I'll do it myself.' She put down her cup and headed for the door. 'I'll make a start right now.'

'Shouldn't you be thinking about your grandmother?' he snapped before she reached it. 'I'm sure she'd appreciate a hot meal when she gets back from the hospital. Or are you so lost to selfishness that you expect her to cook for you?'

'She doesn't…' Then, unexpectedly curbing her tongue, she said, 'I'm not the selfish one around here.'

Annie, aware that in this battle of wits Xandra was her ally, cleared her throat. 'Why don't I get supper?' she offered.

They both turned to stare at her.

'Why would you do that?' George Saxon demanded.

'Because I want my car fixed?'

'You won't get a better offer,' Xandra declared, leaping in before her father could turn down her somewhat rash offer. 'My limit is baked beans on toast. I'm sure Annie can do better than that,' she said, throwing a pleading glance in her direction.

'Can you?' he demanded.

'Do better than baked beans on toast?' she repeated. 'Actually, that won't be…' She broke off, distracted by the wild signals Xandra was making behind her father's back. As he turned to see what had caught her attention she went on. 'Difficult. Not at all.'

He gave her a long look through narrowed eyes, clearly aware that he'd missed something. Then continued to look at her as if there was something about her that bothered him.

She knew just how he felt.

The way he looked at her bothered her to bits, she thought, using her forefinger to push the 'prop' spectacles up her nose. They would keep sliding down, making it easier to look over them than through them, which made wearing them utterly pointless.

'How long do you think it'll take?' she asked, not sure who she was attempting to distract. George or herself.

He continued to stare for perhaps another ten seconds—clearly not a man to be easily distracted—before he shrugged and said, 'It depends what else we find. Your car is not exactly in the first flush. Once something major happens it tends to have a knock-on effect. You're touring, you say?'

She nodded. 'That was the plan. Shropshire, Cheshire, maybe. A little sightseeing. A little shopping.'

'There aren't enough sights, enough shops in London?' he enquired, an edge to his voice that suggested he wasn't entirely convinced.

'Oh, well…' She matched his shrug and raised him a smile. 'You know what they say about a change.'

'Being as good as a rest?' He sounded doubtful. 'This isn't a great time of year to break down, especially if you're stranded miles from anywhere,' he pointed out.

He didn't bother to match her smile.

'It's never a good time for that, George.'

'It's a lot less dangerous when the days are long and the nights warm,' he said, leaving her to imagine what it would be like if she broke down way out in the country, in the dark, with the temperature below freezing. Then, having got that off his chest, 'Are you in a hurry to be anywhere in particular?'

He sounded hopeful.

'Well, no. That's the joy of touring, isn't it? There's no fixed agenda. And now Xandra has told me about the Christmas market in Maybridge this weekend…' she gave another little shrug, mainly because she was certain it would annoy him

'…well, I wouldn't want to miss that.' It was a new experience. Annoying a man. One she could grow to enjoy and, taking full advantage of this opportunity, she mentally crossed her fingers and added, 'Ho, ho, ho…'

That earned her another snort—muffled this time—from Xandra, who got a look to singe her ears from her father before he turned back to her and, ignoring her attempt at levity, asked, 'Have you spoken to your insurance company?'

'Why would I do that?'

'Because you've had an accident?'

'Oh. Yes.' The prospect of contacting her insurance company and what that would mean took all the fun out of winding up George Saxon. 'I suppose I have. It never occurred to me…'

'No?' He gave her another of those thoughtful looks. 'Maybe you should do it now although, bearing in mind the age of the car and the likely cost of repairs, their loss adjuster will probably decide to simply write it off.'

'What? They can't do that!'

'I think you'll find they can.'

'Only if I make a claim.'

He didn't answer. And this time Xandra didn't leap in to defend her.

'I *am* insured,' she said hurriedly, before George asked the question that was clearly foremost in his mind.

She didn't blame him. First she wasn't able to produce her licence and now she didn't want her insurance company involved. Anyone with two brain cells to rub together would believe she had something to hide.

Obviously not whatever scenario was going through his mind right now, but something. And they'd be right to be suspicious.

But she was insured.

She'd checked that Lydia's car was covered by her own insurance policy but now, faced with the reality of accidental damage, she realised that it wasn't that simple. If, on the day she made a claim for an accident in Maybridge, the entire world knew she was flying to Bab el Sama—and they would, because she'd made absolutely sure that the press knew where she was going; she wanted them there, establishing her alibi by snatching shots of 'her' walking on the beach—well, that really would put the cat among the pigeons.

She couldn't tell him that, of course, but she was going to have to tell him something and the longer she delayed, the less likely it was that he would believe her. From being in a position of power, Annie now felt at a distinct disadvantage in the low chair and, putting down her cup, she stood up so that she could look him in the eye.

'You needn't worry that I won't pay you. I have money.' And, determined to establish her financial probity at least, she tugged at the neck of the V-neck sweater she was wearing, reached down inside her shirt and fished a wad of fifty-pound notes from one cup of her bra and placed it on the table.

'Whoa!' Xandra said.

'Will a thousand pounds cover it?' she asked, repeating the performance on the other side before looking up to discover that George was staring at her.

'Go and check the stores to see what spares we have in stock, Xandra,' he said, not taking his eyes off her.

His daughter opened her mouth to protest, then, clearly thinking better of it, stomped out, banging the back door as she went.

For a moment the silence rang in her ears. Then, with a gesture at the pile of banknotes, George said, 'Where did that come from?'

Realising she'd just made things ten times worse, that she was going to have to tell him at least some version of the truth, Annie said, 'It's mine.' He didn't move a muscle. 'Truly. I don't want to use credit cards for the same reason I can't call my insurance company.'

'And why is that?' he asked, stony-faced as a statue.

'It's difficult…'

'No licence, no insurance and a pile of hard cash? I'll say it's difficult. What exactly is your problem, Annie?' he asked. 'Who are you running away from? The police?'

'No! It's nothing like that. It's...' Oh, help...
'It's personal.'

He frowned. 'Are you telling me that it's a
domestic?'

Was he asking her if she was running from an
abusive husband?

'You're not wearing a ring,' he pointed out, forest-
alling the temptation to grab such a perfect cover story.

'No. I'm not married.'

'A partner, then. So why all the subterfuge?' he
said, picking up one of the wads of banknotes,
flicking the edge with his thumb. 'And where did
this come from?'

'My parents left me some money. I daren't use
credit cards—'

'Or claim on your motor insurance.'

She nodded.

'Is he violent?'

'No!'

'But unwilling to let you go.'

She swallowed and he accepted that as an affir-
mative. This was going better than she'd hoped.

'How will he trace you? You understand that I
have to think about Xandra. And my mother.'

'There's a security firm he uses, but they think
I've left the country. As long as I don't do anything
to attract attention, they won't find me.'

'I hope you didn't leave your passport behind.'

'No. The clothes I'm wearing, the car, belong to

the friend who helped me get away,' she said before he asked her why her 'partner' was in the habit of hiring a security firm to keep tabs on her. 'You can understand why I feel so bad about what's happened to the car. Will you be able to fix it?'

He looked at her for a long time before shaking his head. 'I knew you were trouble from the first moment I set eyes on you,' he said, 'and I know I'm going to regret this, but I'll see if your car is salvageable so I can get you on your way. I just hope I don't live to see the name Annie Rowland linked with mine in the headlines.'

'That won't happen,' she promised.

'Of course it won't. The only thing I am sure of where you're concerned is that your name isn't Rowland.'

'It *is* Annie,' she said, glad for some reason that she couldn't begin to fathom that she had chosen to use her own best name.

'Then let's leave it at that,' he said, putting down the mug as he pushed himself away from the table. 'But whatever you plan on cooking for dinner, Annie, had better be worth all the trouble you're causing.'

'I can guarantee that it'll be better than beans on toast,' she promised. 'Thank you for trusting me, George.'

'Who said I trusted you?' He looked at her as if he was going to say more, but let it go. 'Save your thanks and put that out of sight,' he said, pointing at the pile of notes lying on the kitchen table. Then, as she made a move to stuff it back in her bra, 'No! I didn't mean…' He took a deep breath. 'Just wait until I've gone.'

She blushed furiously. 'Sorry.'

'So am I,' he muttered as he left the kitchen. 'So am I.'

CHAPTER FOUR

ANNIE hadn't been aware of holding her breath, but the minute the back door closed she covered her hot cheeks with her hands and let out something very close to a, 'Whew.'

That had been intense.

She appeared to have got away with it, though. For now, at any rate. And she hadn't told any outright lies, just left George to answer his own questions. A bit of a grey area, no doubt, but she was sure he'd rather not know the truth and twenty-four hours from now she'd be miles away from Maybridge with no harm done.

The cat leapt from the chair as she crossed to the fridge, chirruping hopefully as it nuzzled its head against her ankle.

'Hello, puss. Are you hungry too?'

She poured a little milk into a bowl, then sat back on her heels, watching the cat lap it up.

'Trouble,' she said, grinning in spite of everything that had happened. 'He said I was trouble. Do you know, puss, that's the very first time anyone has ever looked at me and thought "trouble".' The cat looked up, milk clinging to its muzzle, and responded with a purr. 'I know,' Annie said. 'It is immensely cheering. Almost worth wrecking Lydia's car for.' Then, since the cat made a very good listener, 'Tell me, would you describe George Saxon as a likely beach bum?'

The cat, stretching out its tongue to lick the last drop from its whiskers, appeared to shake its head.

'No, I didn't think so, either.'

Surely 'laid-back' was the very definition of beach-bum-hood, while George Saxon was, without doubt, the most intense man she'd ever met.

With Xandra on his case, she suspected, he had quite a lot to be intense about, although if he really was an absentee father he undoubtedly deserved it. And what was all that about closing down the garage? How could he do that while his own father was in hospital? It was utterly appalling—and a private family matter that was absolutely none of her business, she reminded herself.

She just wanted to get the car fixed and get back on the road. Take in the sights, go shopping unrecognised. But, despite Xandra's build-up and her assurance that she wouldn't miss it, she'd be giving the Maybridge Christmas market a wide berth.

Less ho, ho, ho… More no, no, no…

The thought made her feel oddly guilty. As if

she'd somehow let the girl down. Which was stupid. If it hadn't been for Xandra, she would have been picked up by some other mechanic who wouldn't have given her nearly as much grief.

A man without the careless arrogance that was guaranteed to rouse any woman with an ounce of spirit to a reckless response. One who wouldn't have held her in a way that made her feel like a woman instead of a piece of porcelain.

Someone polite, who would not have made uncomplimentary comments about her driving, but would have promised to deliver her car in full working order the next day because that was on the customer relations script he'd learned on his first day on the job.

In other words, all the things that she wanted to get away from.

Whatever else George was, he certainly didn't follow a script. And locking horns with a man who didn't know he was supposed to show due deference to the nation's sweetheart was a lot more interesting than being holed up in a budget hotel room with only the television remote for company.

For all his faults, George Saxon did have one thing in his favour—he was the complete opposite of Rupert Devenish, a man who had never rated a single 'whew'. Not from her, anyway.

There was nothing textbook about George.

Okay, so he was tall, with shoulders wide enough

to fill a doorway—no doubt like the lines carved into his cheeks, around those penetrating grey eyes, they came from hard use.

And he was dark.

But he wasn't, by any stretch of the imagination, classically handsome. On the contrary, his face had a lived-in quality and there was enough stubble on his chin to suggest a certain laissez-faire attitude to his appearance. He certainly wasn't a man to wait for some woman to pluck him off the 'ideal husband' shelf, she thought. More the kind who, when he saw what he wanted, would act like a caveman.

The thought, which was supposed to make her smile, instead prompted the proverbial ripple down her spine. Something which, until today, she'd foolishly imagined to be no more than a figure of speech.

He was, by any standard, anything but ideal and she had the strongest feeling that her wisest course of action would be to make his day and get out of there, fast.

But, then again, why would she when, for the purposes of this adventure, he could almost have been made to order.

Exciting, annoying, disturbing.

She'd wanted to be disturbed, jolted out of her rut. Wanted to be excited and, maybe, just a little bit reckless.

She swallowed as she considered what being reckless with George Saxon would entail.

He was right. She should definitely leave. As soon as possible. Not because the idea appalled her. On the contrary, it was much too excitingly disturbing, recklessly appealing and she'd call a taxi to take her to the motel.

Just as soon as she'd cooked the hot meal she'd promised them.

Her stomach rumbled at the thought. Lunch had been a very long time ago and she'd been too nervous to eat more than a mouthful of that. Not that she'd eaten much of anything lately, a fact that had been picked up by one of the gossip magazines looking for a new angle. An eating disorder was always good copy.

Now, for the first time in months, she felt genuinely hungry and, leaving the cat to its ablutions, she stood up and returned her attention to the fridge.

It was well stocked with the basics, but it wasn't just the bacon, eggs, cheese and vegetables that were making her hungry. She'd already seen the large homemade meat pie sitting on the middle shelf, gravy oozing gently from the slit in the centre, just waiting to be slipped into the oven.

Presumably it had been made by George's mother before she'd left to visit her husband in the hospital. That Xandra knew it was there was obvious from her earlier performance but, anxious to keep her grandfather's garage functioning, desperate, maybe, to prove herself to her father, she was prepared to take any chance that came her way and she'd grabbed her offer to make dinner for them all with both hands.

Good for her, she thought. If you had a dream you shouldn't let anyone talk you out of it, or stand in your way. You should go for it with all your heart.

Annie put the pie in the oven, then set about the task of peeling potatoes and carrots. It took her a minute or two to get the hang of the peeler, then, as she bent to her task, the annoying glasses slid down her nose and fell into the sink.

She picked them out of the peelings and left them on the draining board while she finished.

Her only problem then was the vexed question of how long it took potatoes to boil. She'd left her handbag in the car, but she'd put her cellphone in her coat pocket after calling for help. She wiped her hands and dug it out to see what she could find on the Web.

The minute she switched it on she got the 'message waiting' icon.

There was a text from Lydia with just a single code word to reassure her that everything had gone exactly according to plan, that she'd reached the airport without problem—or, as she'd put it, being twigged as a 'ringer'.

Even if they hadn't agreed that contact between them should be on an emergency-only basis—you never knew who was tuned into a cellphone frequency—she'd still be in the air so she couldn't call her and tell her everything that had happened, confess to having cut her hair, wrecking her car. Instead, she keyed in the agreed response, confirmation that she, too, was okay, and hit 'send'.

There was, inevitably, a voicemail from her grandfather asking her to call and let him know when she'd touched down safely. Using any excuse to override her insistence that she wanted to be left completely alone while she was away.

'You'll have to call me at King's Lacey,' he said. 'I'm going there tomorrow to start preparations for Christmas.' Piling on yet more guilt. 'And the Boxing Day shoot.'

As if he didn't have a housekeeper, a gamekeeper, a houseful of staff who were perfectly capable of doing all that without him.

'And of course there's the Memorial Service. It will be twenty years this year and I want it to be special. You will be home for that?'

It was the unexpected touch of uncertainty in his voice that finally got to her.

'I'll be there,' she murmured to herself, holding the phone to her chest long after the voicemail had ended.

It was twenty years since her parents had died in a hail of gunfire in the week before Christmas and every year she'd relived that terrible intermingling of grief and celebration that made the season an annual misery.

And worse, much worse, the centuries-old Boxing Day shoot that nothing was allowed to interfere with. Not even that first year. Cancelling it would have been letting her parents' killers win, her grandfather had said when he'd found her hiding beneath the stairs, hands over her ears in terror as the guns had blasted away.

'God help me,' she said again, 'I'll be there.'

Then she straightened, refusing to waste another minute dwelling on it. Having come so close to losing this little bit of freedom, she was absolutely determined to make the most of every moment. Even something as simple, as unusual for her, as cooking dinner. But as she clicked to the Net to surf for cooking times, the sound of something hitting the floor made her jump practically out of her skin.

She spun round and saw George Saxon in the doorway, her bag at his feet.

How long had he been there? How much had he heard?

George hadn't intended to eavesdrop, but when he'd opened the door Annie had been half turned from him, so tense, the cellphone so tight to her ear that she hadn't noticed him and he'd frozen, unable to advance or retreat.

He'd heard her promise to 'be there', but the 'God help me…' that had followed as she'd clutched the phone to her chest had been so deeply felt that any doubts about the kind of trouble she was in vanished as, for a moment, all control had slipped away and she'd looked simply desolate.

At that moment he'd wanted only to reach out to her, hold her. Which was when he'd dropped her bag at his feet.

And she'd visibly jumped.

'I'm sorry,' he said. 'I didn't mean to startle you.' Just shatter the spell that she seemed to be weaving around him.

'You didn't,' she said, a little too fiercely. Then blushed at the lie. 'Well, maybe just a bit.'

She looked down at the cellphone, then crammed it quickly into the back pocket of her jeans. Unlike her clothes or the holdall he'd just brought in from the car, which was definitely from the cheap-and-cheerful, market-stall end of the spectrum, it was the latest in expensive, top-end technology. He had one exactly like it himself and knew how much it had cost. And he wondered what kind of wardrobe she'd left behind in London, along with her driving licence, when she'd made her bid for freedom.

A woman whose partner could afford to employ a security company to keep an eye on her would be dressed from her skin up in designer labels. Silk, linen, cashmere. Would wear fine jewels.

What had he done to her to make her run? If not physical, then mental cruelty because she was running away from him, not to someone. His hands bunched into fists at the thought.

'I was just catching up on my messages,' she said.

'Nothing you wanted to hear, by the look of you.' For a moment she stared at him as if she wanted to say something, then shook her head. 'You do know that you can be tracked by your phone signal?' he asked.

Not that it was any of his business, he reminded himself, forcing his hands to relax.

'It was only for a minute. I need to know what's happening.'

Long enough. Who was important enough to her that she'd take the risk? Make that kind of promise?

A child?

No. She'd never have left a child behind.

'Use some of that money you've got stashed away to buy the anonymity of a pay-as-you-go,' he advised abruptly.

'I will,' she said, clearly as anxious as he was to change the subject. Then, lifting her chin, managing a smile, 'I found a pie in the fridge so I've put that in the oven. I hope that's all right?'

'A pie?'

'A meat pie.'

'Ah…'

A tiny crease puckered the space between her beautifully arched brows.

'Is that a good "ah" or a bad "ah"?' she asked. Then, raising her hand to her mouth to display a set of perfectly manicured nails, she said, 'Please don't tell me you're a vegetarian.'

'Why?' he demanded. 'Have you got something against vegetarians?'

'No, but…'

'Relax. You're safe. What you've found is the equivalent of the fatted calf…'

'I'm sorry?'

'For the prodigal son.'

'I'm familiar with the metaphor.' She regarded him intently. 'Just how long is it since you've been home?' she asked.

'A while,' he said.

Which was why his mother, even with his father in hospital, had taken the time to make him one of her special steak-and-mushroom pies, just as she'd been doing ever since he'd gone away on his first school trip. More to avoid his own sense of guilt than tease her, he said, 'Judging by your reaction, I suspect we've both had something of a narrow escape.'

'Escape?' Annie, swiftly recovering from whatever had upset her, placed a hand against her breast in a gesture perfectly calculated to mime shocked surprise and said, 'Are you suggesting that I can't cook, Mr Saxon?'

Despite everything, he found himself grinning at

her performance. 'I sensed a lack of conviction in your assurance that you could do better than Xandra.'

'That was no more than simple modesty,' she declared.

'You'll forgive me if I reserve judgement until I've tasted your mashed potatoes.'

'Mashed?' The insouciant air vanished as quickly as it had come. 'Is that another favourite?'

'Food for the gods,' he assured her. 'At least it is the way my mother makes it.'

'Well, I'm not your mother, for which I'm deeply grateful since you appear to be as casual a son as you are a father, but I'll do my best not to disappoint.' Then, as he scowled at her, 'I don't suppose you've any idea how long it takes to boil potatoes?'

Which suggested he'd been right about the narrow escape.

'Sorry. That's not my area of expertise.'

'No?' She lifted those expressive brows, inviting him to tell her what he was an expert in, then, when he didn't oblige, she gave a little shrug and said, 'I don't suppose there's a lot of call for potato mashing on the beach.'

'You know how it is with sand,' he replied, wondering what kind of woman didn't know how to cook something as basic as potatoes.

The kind who'd never had to cook, obviously. Or close car doors behind her.

Who the devil *was* she?

'It gets in everything?' she offered. Then, because there really wasn't anything else to say about potatoes, 'Thanks for bringing in my bag.'

'I didn't make a special journey,' he said and, irritated with himself for getting drawn into conversation, he took a glass from the dresser and crossed to the sink to fill it.

'Thirsty work?' she asked, watching him as he drained it.

'No matter how much water I drink on long-haul flights, I still seem to get dehydrated.'

'Excuse me?'

He glanced back at her as he refilled the glass.

'Are you telling me that you flew from California *today*?' she demanded, clearly horrified.

'Overnight. I slept most of the way,' he assured her. The first-class sky-bed he could afford these days was a very different experience from his early cattle-class flights.

'Even so, you shouldn't be working with machinery. What about Health and Safety?'

'Goods and Services, Health and Safety? What are you, Annie? A lawyer?'

'Just a concerned citizen.'

'Is that so? Well, if you don't tell, I won't,' he replied flippantly, refusing to think about how long it had been since anyone, apart from his mother, had been concerned about him. It was his choice, he reminded himself.

'I'm serious,' she said, not in the least bit amused. 'I wouldn't forgive myself if you were hurt fixing my car. It can wait until tomorrow.'

'You're *that* concerned?' Then, because the thought disturbed him more than he liked, 'Don't worry, I'm only there in a supervisory capacity. Xandra's doing all the hard work.'

'Is that supposed to make me feel better?'

'It's supposed to make you feel grateful,' he said, determined to put an end to the conversation and get out of there. 'Since you're so eager to be on your way.' Then, as he noticed her glasses lying on the draining board, he frowned. 'And actually,' he said thoughtfully as he picked them up and, realising that they were wet and muddy, rinsed them under the tap, 'I'm hoping a taste of the real thing will encourage her to reconsider a career as a motor mechanic and finish school.'

'Always a good plan,' Annie agreed. 'How old is she?'

'Sixteen.'

He picked up a dish cloth and, having dried the frames, began to polish the lenses.

'In that case, she doesn't have much choice in the matter. She can't leave school until she's seventeen.'

'I know that. You know that. Which may go some way to explain why she went to so much trouble to get herself suspended from her boarding school.'

Annie frowned. 'She's at boarding school?'

'Dower House.'

'I see.'

She could sympathise with her father's lack of enthusiasm at her career choice after he'd sent her to one of the most expensive boarding schools in the country. The kind that turned out female captains of industry, politicians, women who changed the world. The school where, two years ago, she'd given the end-of-year address to the girls, had presented the prizes.

She clearly hadn't made that much of an impression on young Xandra Saxon. Or maybe the haircut was worse than she thought.

'Obviously she's not happy there.'

'I wanted the best for her. I live in the States and, as you may have gathered, her mother is easily distracted. It seems that she's on honeymoon at the moment.'

'Her third,' Annie said, remembering what Xandra had said.

'Second. We didn't have one. I was a first-year student with a baby on the way when we got married.'

'That must have been tough,' she said.

'It wasn't much fun for either of us,' he admitted. 'Penny went home to her mother before Xandra was due and she never came back. I don't blame her. When I wasn't studying, I was working every hour just to keep us fed and housed. It wasn't what she'd expected from the son of George Saxon.'

'I'm sorry.'

'So am I.'

Then, because he clearly didn't want to talk about it and she didn't much want to hear about a youthful marriage that appeared never to have had a chance, she said, 'So, what did she do? Xandra. To get herself suspended.'

'She borrowed the head's car and took it for a joyride.'

'Ouch.' Sixteen years old, so she wouldn't have a licence or insurance. That explained a lot. 'Attention-seeking?'

'Without much success. Presumably anticipating something of the sort, Penny had the foresight to switch off her cellphone.'

'Then it's just as well Xandra has you.'

His smile was of the wry, self-deprecating kind. 'I'm the last person she'd have called, Annie. Much as I would have wished it otherwise, I'm little more to my daughter than a signature on a cheque.'

'You think so?'

George held the spectacles up to the light to check, amongst other things, that they were smear-free before looking at Annie.

'I know so. I'm only here because my father had a heart attack,' he said, taking a step towards her and, as she looked up, he slipped her spectacles back on her nose, holding them in place for a moment, his thumbs against the cool skin stretched taut over fine cheekbones.

Her lips parted on a tiny gasp but she didn't protest or pull away from him and for what seemed like an eternity he simply cradled her face.

There was no sound. Nothing moved.

Only the dark centre at the heart of eyes that a man might drown in widened to swallow the dazzling blue. He'd have had to be made of ice to resist such a blatant invitation, but then, according to any number of women he'd known, he was ice to the bone…

'The first rule of wearing a disguise, Annie…' he began, touching his lips briefly to hers to prove, if only to himself, that he was immune.

Discovering, too late, that he was not.

CHAPTER FIVE

ANNIE'S lips were soft, yielding, as they parted on a little gasp of surprise. Not the response of a seductress bent on luring a man to his doom, he thought, more the reaction of a girl being kissed for the first time.

Arousing in a way that no practised kiss could ever be.

And when, slightly breathless, he drew back to look at her, her eyes were closed and the mouth that had tempted him to take such outrageous liberties was smiling as if it had discovered something brand-new.

'The first rule of wearing a disguise,' he tried again, his voice barely audible as he struggled not to kiss her again, 'is never to let it slip, even for a moment.'

It took a moment for his words to get past the haze of desire but then her eyes flew open and he felt the heat beneath his fingertips as colour seared her cheekbones. Whether at the way she'd responded to his touch or at being found out in her deception, he'd have been hard put to say.

'H-how did you know?' she asked, making no

effort to put distance between them, which appeared to answer that question. The innocent blushes had to be as fake as her glasses.

'Since you weren't wearing them when you checked your messages, it seemed likely that they were purely for decoration,' he said.

'Decoration?' The beginnings of a smile tugged once more at the corners of her mouth. 'Hardly that.'

'I've seen prettier,' he admitted, struggling not to smile back.

'The wretched things fell into the potato peelings. I put them on the draining board and then forgot all about them.'

As clear an admission of guilt as he'd ever heard.

'You should have tossed them into the bin with the peelings.'

'I doubt they'd have added much to the compost heap.'

'Maybe not, but if you're afraid of being recognised, I'd advise getting yourself a pair that fits properly instead of sliding down your nose.' He waited, hoping that she might tell him the truth this time. 'Maybe go for tinted lenses.'

Something to tone down the distracting blue.

'I bought them on the Internet. I had no idea they came in different sizes.' She gave a little shrug. 'Maybe I should get some little sexy ones with lenses that react to the light.'

'Maybe. I have to tell you, though, that if anyone has put together a photofit of you, you can forget the glasses. It's the hairdo that's the dead giveaway.'

'Oh…' she lifted a hand to her hair in a self-conscious gesture '…no. No danger there.' She pulled a face. 'I cut it myself this morning with a pair of nail scissors.'

Well, yes. Obviously. No woman would walk around with hair like that for a minute longer than she had to.

'I'd have bet on the garden shears,' he said, accepting that she wasn't going to trust him with her secret. Or was, perhaps, protecting him from something he was almost certainly better off not knowing?

Just as he'd be wiser not to imagine how her hair might have looked before she'd hacked it off.

Adding long, creamy-coloured silky hair to the image that was building up inside his head was not helping him drop his hands, take the necessary step back.

'I'd better get back,' he said, forcing himself to do just that. 'Before Xandra, in her enthusiasm, strips your car down to the frame.'

He picked up the glass of water he'd abandoned but at the door he stopped, looked back. Despite a natural poise, a look-him-in-the-eye assurance that was so at odds with her innocent blushes, there was a lack of knowingness in the way she'd responded to his kiss that didn't quite fit with the jealous-partner scenario.

But then, presumably, if she was any kind of con woman, she'd have that down pat.

When the silence, the look, had gone on for too long, he said, 'You might find the answer to the vexed question of how to boil a potato in one of my mother's cook books. They're over there, behind the television.' He didn't bother to check that they were still there. Nothing had been changed in this room in his lifetime. 'And, in case you're interested, I'm partial to a touch of garlic in my mash.'

'Garlic?' She pushed the glasses, already sliding down her nose again, back into place. 'Good choice,' she said. 'Very good for the heart, garlic.'

'Are you suggesting that mine needs help?'

'Actually, I was thinking about your father. Isn't heart disease supposed to be hereditary? Although, now you come to mention it, maybe yours could do with some work in other departments.'

'What makes you think that?' He wasn't arguing with her conclusion, merely interested in her reasoning.

'Well, let me see. Could it be because you're the one with your daughter up to her elbows in axle-grease while you stand back telling her what to do?'

The smile that went with this, reassurance that she was teasing, was no mere token but shone out of her, lighting up her face in a way that could make a man forget that she was too thin. Forget the hair. Forget anything…

'I'm not telling her anything. She wasn't exaggerating when she said she knew what she was doing.'

Her smile became a look of sympathy. 'That must be a worry.'

'My father never forgave me for not wanting to follow him into the business. Given a second chance with Xandra, it's clear that he hasn't made the same mistakes with her that he did with me.'

Or maybe, being a girl, she'd had to beg to be allowed to 'play' cars with her granddad.

He wondered if his old man had seen the irony in that. Probably not. He'd doted on Xandra since the moment she'd been born. Indulged her, as he'd never been indulged. Maybe that was the difference between being a father and a grandfather. There was not the same responsibility to be perfect, do everything right. And getting it wrong.

'She might just love it,' Annie pointed out.

'I'm sure she does, but there's a world of difference between doing something for fun in the school holidays and it being your only option.'

'So if she stayed at school, took her exams, went to university and at the end of it all she still wanted to be a garage mechanic?' she asked.

'If only. She wants to drive rally cars too.' He took a deep breath. 'I don't suppose you have a handy Health and Safety regulation you're prepared to quote on the subject of sixteen-year-olds doing dangerous jobs?'

'I don't have one on the tip of my tongue,' she said, 'but, even if I did, I don't think I'd use it.'

'Not even if I promised to fix your car myself?'

'Not even then. This is something she wants, George. Something she can do. That she believed no one would take away from her.'

'That sounded heartfelt.'

'Yes, well, at her age I had a dream of my own, but I allowed myself to be persuaded against it for what at the time seemed sound reasons. Not that I believe Xandra is going to be the walkover I was. She's nowhere near as eager to please.'

'A daddy's girl, were you?'

She paled, shook her head, but before he could take a step back towards her, say sorry even though he didn't know why, she said, 'You do realise that if you close the garage it will make her all the more determined?'

'It's not an option. No matter how much he fights it, the truth is that my father won't be able to carry on.'

'What about you? This is your chance to prove to your daughter that you're more than just a signature on a cheque. That you really care about what she wants. Or is there a Californian beach with a Californian beach girl stretched out in the sun who you can't wait to get back to?' She didn't wait for an answer but, having planted that little bombshell, said, 'I'll give you a call when dinner's ready, shall I?'

'Do that,' he snapped, turning abruptly and leaving her to it.

Annie didn't move until she heard the outside door close. Only then did she raise her hands to her face, run her fingertips over the warm spots where George Saxon had touched her.

He'd been so close as he'd slipped the glasses on her nose, held them in place, his thumbs against her cheek, fingertips supporting her head. There had been an intimacy about the way he'd looked at her that had warmed her, made her pulse leap, stirred something deep inside her so that when his lips had touched hers it had felt like two pieces of a puzzle finding the perfect fit.

And if he could do that with a look, a touch, a tender kiss, what could he do if…?

She whirled around, refusing to go there.

Instead, she crossed to the corner to root through the small collection of old cookery books before pulling out a heavy black bound book that was re-assuringly familiar.

She'd kept all her mother's books—medical textbooks, mostly—and a copy of this basic cookery book had been among them, the inscription on the flyleaf from the foster mother who'd taught her to cook and passed on her own cookery book when she'd left for university.

How much strength of will must it have taken her mother to get to medical school? More than she'd had, she thought, swallowing hard as she opened the book to check the index.

Potatoes…

Potatoes, it seemed, took around twenty minutes to boil, depending on whether they were old or new and, once cooked, should be creamed with a little pepper and margarine. Clearly post-war austerity had still been part of life when this book had been published. And a sprinkle of parsley was as exotic as it got back in the days when garlic was considered dangerously foreign.

But, despite the fact that Mrs Saxon's cookery book and fridge appeared to be from the same generation, the large bulb of garlic tucked away in the salad crisper suggested that she, at least, had moved with the times. Or had that been bought specially for the prodigal's homecoming too?

She laid the table, put plates to warm and was energetically mashing butter, milk and finely chopped garlic into the potatoes when she heard the kitchen door open.

'Perfect timing,' she said, concentrating on the job in hand. 'Just enough time to scrub up.' Then, when there was no answer, she turned round. 'Oh!' Not George or Xandra, but a slender middle-aged woman who bore a clear resemblance to both of them. 'Mrs Saxon,' she said, wiping her hands on the apron she'd found hanging behind the door and offering her hand. 'I'm Annie Rowland. I hope you don't mind me making free with your kitchen, but George thought you'd be tired when you got back from the hospital. How is your husband?'

'As bad-tempered as any man who's being told to change the habits of a lifetime and give up everything he loves…'

Before she could say any more, Xandra burst through the door and flung her arms around her grandmother.

'Gran! How's Granddad?'

'He'll be fine. He just needs to take more care of himself. But what about you, young lady? What are you doing here? Why aren't you at school?' Then, clearly knowing her granddaughter better than most, 'I suppose it's got something to do with your mother?'

'I don't care about my mother. I just wanted to be here so that I can help Granddad with the garage.'

'Oh, Xandra!' Then, with a sigh, 'What have you done?'

'You didn't know she was here?' George asked, following his daughter into the kitchen and this time he'd been getting his hands dirty—presumably in an effort to get the job done as quickly as possible so that he could get rid of her and close down the garage.

'I would have mentioned it.'

'You've a lot on your plate.' He crossed to the sink and, squishing soap on his hands, began to wash them thoroughly. 'How are things at the hospital?'

'It would help if he wasn't fretting so much. The garage is his life.'

'He's going to have to widen his horizons.' He picked up a towel. 'If it's any help, tell him I'll take care of the Bentley myself,' he said, drying his hands. 'But I'll have to get in touch with the owner of the restoration job in the end bay. The baby Austin. He'll need to start looking for another garage—'

'It's mine,' Xandra cut in with a touch of defiance as she anticipated disapproval.

George frowned. 'Yours?'

'Granddad bought it for my birthday,' she said, swiftly bending to make a fuss of the cat, as if she knew she'd just thrown a hand grenade into the room. 'It's a restoration project. We've been doing it together.'

No one else was looking at George and only she saw the effect that had on him. As if he'd been hit, winded, all the air driven from his body. A big man destroyed by a few words from a slip of a girl.

Love, she thought. Only love could hurt you like that and she ached to go to him, hold him.

'I'll go and give Mike Jackson a call about the Bentley,' his mother said, oblivious to the tension— or perhaps choosing to ignore it. 'He's got a wedding next week and I know how worried he's been.'

'I'll do it,' George said, clearly needing to get out of the room for a moment. 'I need to talk to him.' Then his eyes met hers and in an instant the barriers were back up. Nothing showing on the surface. 'Sorry, Mum, I should have introduced Annie.'

'We've met.' Mrs Saxon turned to her with a smile. 'I'm so sorry, my dear. I didn't thank you for getting on with dinner.' She patted her arm distractedly. 'We'll talk later but right now I really must go and call my sister-in-law, let her know how her brother is. Xandra, come and say hello to Great-Aunt Sarah.'

Annie wanted to say something, talk about Xandra, ask him what had gone wrong, but this didn't come under polite conversation and she had no idea where to begin.

As if sensing the danger, George crossed to the stove, hooked his finger through the mash and tasted it.

'Not bad for a first effort,' he said.

'Not bad? I'll have you know I've eaten in some of the finest restaurants in London and that stands comparison with the best.'

'Which restaurants?'

Annie had reeled off the names of half a dozen of the most expensive restaurants in the capital in her absolute determination to impress him before she realised that she was giving away rather more than she'd ever intended.

He lifted a quizzical brow. 'What was that you were saying about modesty?'

She pulled a face. 'No point in being coy. Of course you'd only get a tiny spoonful.'

'The more you pay, the less you get,' he agreed, taking a second dip in the potato. 'Maybe that's why you're so thin. You'd have been better occupied doing a little home cooking and saving your money for a more roadworthy car for your getaway.'

She rapped his knuckles sharply with a spoon and having scooped the potato into a serving bowl, bent to put it in the warming oven.

George regarded her thoughtfully for a moment before he shrugged and said, 'How long has your friend had that sorry heap?' he asked.

'Are you referring to Lydia's pride and joy? Only a week or two,' she said, concentrating on straining the carrots and peas. Then, realising that it wasn't an idle question, 'You've found something else?'

'I don't suppose there's the faintest chance that she bought it from a garage that offered her some kind of warranty?' he asked.

'No. She bought it from a woman who was going to use the money to take her grandchildren on holiday for Christmas.'

Lydia had been eager to tell her all about the one careful lady owner when she'd offered to lend it to her. Pride of ownership coming through loud and clear as she'd explained that, although her car wasn't new, it had been well cared for.

'She didn't happen to be a vicar's wife too, by any chance?'

'Excuse me?'

He sighed. 'Did she see any documents? Service record, receipt? Did this kindly grandmother invite her into her house for tea and biscuits while they did the deal or did your friend buy it off the side of the road?'

'I don't know about the documents, but I do know that the woman lived on the other side of London so she offered to bring the car to Lydia to save her the journey.'

'How kind of her.' His intonation suggested she had been anything but kind and he underlined it by saying, 'She must have thought it was her birthday and Christmas all rolled into one.'

'I don't understand.'

'Your friend was sold a cut'n'shut, Annie. A car welded together out of two wrecks. The front half of one car and the back half of another.'

She shook her head. 'That can't be right. She'd bought it new—'

'The classic "one careful lady owner".' He shook his head. 'Your sweet little old lady sold your friend a deathtrap, Annie. If that abomination had come apart while you were driving at any speed…'

He left the outcome to her imagination.

Her imagination, in full working order, duly obliged with a rerun of the carefree way she'd driven down the motorway, relishing her freedom as she'd buzzed along in the fast lane, overtaking slower moving traffic.

All it would have taken at that speed would have been a small piece of debris, a bit of a bump and she could have ended up in the path of one of the lorries thundering west…

And if it hadn't been her, it would, sooner or later, have been Lydia.

'Xandra hadn't seen one before but, when she spotted the welding, she asked me to take a look.'

So that was how he'd got his hands dirty.

'You do understand what this means? It'll have to be crushed. I can't be responsible for letting it back on the road.'

'Crushed?' Right now, she would be glad never to see it again but—

'And any documentation that came with it will be fake,' he added pointedly. 'This would be a good time to come clean if you've been economical with the truth about the car's provenance, since I will have to inform the Driver and Vehicle Licensing Agency.' His look was long and intense, demanding an answer.

'I've got the picture, George.'

'I can leave it a day or two if it's going to be a problem?' he pressed.

It wasn't necessary, but her heart did a little loop the loop that he was prepared to cover for her. Give her getaway time.

'Thanks, but I won't strain your probity, George. The car is properly registered in the name of Lydia Young. She's the only victim here.' Then she groaned. 'Lydia! She's spent all that money on something that's absolutely worthless.' She looked up at him. 'I imagine the question of insurance no longer arises?'

He shook his head and she let slip that new word she was finding all kinds of uses for, but it didn't help. This went far beyond a slightly shocking expletive.

'How could anyone do such a wicked thing?' she asked.

'For money, Annie.' He made a move as if to put his hand on her arm in a gesture of comfort, but instead lifted it to push his fingers through his thick, dark hair. 'This is going to totally screw up your plans, isn't it?'

'I didn't actually have anything as organised as a plan,' she admitted. 'Just a general direction.'

'Running blind is never a good idea.' Then, almost, it seemed, against his will, 'What will you do now?'

She lifted her shoulders in a resigned shrug. 'Call a cab and go to the motel.' She managed a wry smile. 'Spend the evening working on a plan.'

'Have something to eat first,' he said.

'Thank you. Both of you,' she added. 'I mean that. I'm really grateful that you were so thorough.'

'George Saxon and Son might not look much at the moment, but it was the finest garage in the area for nearly a century.'

'Until it ran out of sons.'

'Until it ran out of sons who wanted to be a replica of their father.'

'It's an equal-opportunities world, George.'

'Actually, when I asked what you're going to do, I meant without a car.'

Then, as Xandra returned, he leaned back against the table and folded his arms, rather like a shield, she thought.

'You'll be stranded on the wrong side of the ring road at the motel,' he said, 'and taxis aren't cheap.'

'Isn't there a bus service?'

'One or two a day, maybe, but it's a motel,' he pointed out. 'A motor hotel. There isn't a lot of demand for public transport.'

'Annie could stay here tonight,' Xandra intervened, in just the same casual manner as she'd handed her the door key and invited her to make herself a cup of tea.

George looked at the girl with something close to exasperation.

'What?' she demanded. 'There's plenty of room and Gran won't mind.'

That he did couldn't have been more obvious.

'I think your grandmother has quite enough to cope with at the moment without taking in a total stranger,' Annie said, rescuing him. 'But thank you for the offer.'

She took her cellphone from her back pocket but, before she could switch it on, he took it from her with a warning look.

'Actually,' he said, 'it would be easier if you stayed here. I'll need you to deal with the paperwork in the morning.' Then, 'I'll have more than enough to do without driving over to the motel.'

She doubted that, but she knew better than to take advantage of a man who'd been put in an impossible position. Even if he had taken advantage of her and kissed her.

'No, really. You've done enough.'

'True,' he said distantly, returning her phone, 'but I've no doubt you'll be the perfect guest and help with the washing-up.'

That really was too much.

'Maybe you should be the perfect son and buy your mother a dishwasher,' she replied, responding in kind.

'Sorry. I flunked that one years ago.' Then, as the door opened behind him, 'You've no objection to Annie staying, have you, Mum?'

'Where else would she go?' Then, as Annie placed the pie and vegetables on the table and she sank wearily into a chair, the phone began to ring.

'I'll go, Gran,' Xandra said, leaping up.

'No… It might be the hospital.'

George followed her from the room but was back in seconds. 'It's one of my mother's friends. She said to start without her.'

'We can wait.'

'The way she's settled herself in the armchair, I suspect it's going to be a long one. No point in letting good food spoil.'

She ducked her head in an attempt to hide the blush that coloured her cheekbones at the simple compliment and, despite everything, he felt an answering warmth as he watched her cut into the pie. She was such a mixture of contradictions.

Assertive, poised, innocent…

She handed him a plate, then, as he helped himself to vegetables, she served Xandra and herself before putting the dishes back in the warming oven for his mother.

Xandra made a deeply appreciative moaning noise. 'Real food. This is worth getting grounded for.'

'It is good,' Annie said swiftly, presumably to stop him from saying something inflammatory. Then spoiled it all by adding, 'For pastry like this I'd come home every week.'

'Once a year would be nearer the mark,' Xandra said.

'Are you suggesting it's up to the standard of all those smart London restaurants you're used to?' he enquired, pretending he hadn't heard. 'Always assuming they served anything as basic as meat pie and mashed potato.'

'It's absolutely delicious,' she said quickly, in an attempt to rescue the blunder. 'But then I can't actually remember the last time I was this hungry.'

From the way she was tucking in, it was clear that her thinness wasn't the result of a desire to be size zero and he wondered what, exactly, she'd been going through that had driven her to fly from home. And, more to the point, who she'd made that *'I'll be there'* promise to.

The one with the desperate *'God help me'* tag.

He pushed away the thought, not wanting to go there.

For the moment there was colour in her cheeks and, as she laughed out loud at something Xandra had said, her face was animated, alive. Then, as if she could sense his eyes on her, she turned, looked at him over those ridiculous frames.

The impact was almost physical.

Forget the fact that she was too thin, that dark smudges marred the porcelain-fine skin beneath her eyes.

It wasn't that instant belt-in-the-gut sexual attraction that normally grabbed his attention and he was honest enough to admit that if he'd passed her in the street, head down, he probably wouldn't have given her a second glance.

But he didn't believe for a minute that she'd ever walk along a street with her head down.

Despite that oddly disturbing vulnerability, she possessed a rare presence, an ability to look him straight in the eye, hold her own in a confrontation.

Not the kind of woman, he'd have said, to run away from anything.

He pushed back his chair the minute he'd finished eating. 'I'd better go and put Mike Jackson out of his misery,' he said, desperate to get away from Annie's unsettling presence. He made a general gesture that took in the table. 'Thanks for doing this…'

'I was glad to help.' She continued to hold him captive with nothing more than a look for what felt like endless seconds. 'Can I get you anything else?' she asked as he lingered.

What on earth was the matter with him?

Annie was the kind of woman that no man with an atom of sense would get entangled with, especially not one who, having learned his lesson the hard way, could spot trouble a mile off.

'Coffee?' she prompted.

'If I need anything I'll get it myself,' he said, forcing himself to move.

CHAPTER SIX

ANNIE felt the tension evaporate as George left the room, but it felt surprisingly empty too. He was very contained, with a rare stillness. He made no unnecessary movements, had been terse to the point of rudeness throughout supper. And yet his presence still filled the room.

What could have happened to cause such a rift between him and his family? Was it just the garage, or had a teenage wedding that had evidently fallen apart faster than the ink had dried on the marriage certificate been the real cause of family friction?

And what about his daughter who, now that her father had left the room, had slumped down in her chair, all that chippy bravado gone.

It was obvious that she craved his attention. She might take every chance to wound her father, but when he wasn't looking her eyes followed him with a kind of desperation.

'Can I suggest something?'

The only response was a shrug of those narrow

shoulders, making her look more like a sulky six-year-old than sixteen.

'Write a note to Mrs Warburton.'

She was instantly back on the defensive. 'I'm not sorry for taking the car.'

'Maybe not, but you're old enough to know that you must have given her a very nasty fright.' She waited a moment but, getting no response, said, 'Why did you do it?'

'Because I could?' she offered, giving her the same barbed I-don't-care-what-you-think-of-me stare that she used to hurt her father and she felt a pang of tenderness for the girl.

'If you wanted to come home to see your father I'm sure she would have understood.'

'I didn't! It's got nothing to do with him!' She glared at her. 'I'll write when I'm ready, okay? If I'd known you were going to nag I wouldn't have asked you to stay.'

'You're right,' she said, standing up, gathering the dishes. 'I've abused your hospitality.' Then, 'Time to wash up, I think.'

'Oh, right. Wash the dishes? Write a letter?' Xandra held out her hands as if balancing the choice. 'Very subtle.'

'The two have a lot in common. They both need doing and neither gets easier for leaving. And I'll bet I'm an amateur in the nagging stakes compared with your gran. As for your father…'

'If he cared what I did he'd be here instead of sending me off to school so that he could live on a beach,' she declared sullenly. 'He might be able to fix it so that they'll take me back, but I won't stay so he might as well save his money.'

'Where do you want to go?'

'Maybridge High School. It was good enough for him. I'll stay here with Gran. She'll need help,' she said. Then, leaping from her chair, she grabbed the bag that George had dropped. 'I'll take this upstairs.'

'Where are you rushing off to?' her grandmother asked as she rushed past her.

'I'm taking Annie's bag up to her room.'

'I've made up the front right bedroom,' she said. 'You'll have to make your own bed.' Then, giving her a quick hug, 'Your granddad will be all right.'

'Of course he will,' she said tightly. 'I'm going to bed.'

'Sleep tight.'

She turned to Annie with a shake of her head. 'I suppose this is about her mother getting married again. The woman doesn't have a thought in her head for anyone but herself.'

'I'd have said it was more to do with her father. She did know he was coming home?'

'I told her when I rang to let her know that her granddad was in hospital. George has always tried to do his best for Xandra, a fact that her mother has used to her own advantage, but it's never been easy and, since she hit her teens…'

'It's a difficult time.'

'And they are so alike. George has probably told you that he and his father had a difficult relationship. It's like watching history repeat itself.'

'I'm sorry to put you to so much trouble when you've already got so much on your plate,' she said, taking the food from the warming oven and placing it on the table.

'What trouble?' she said with a smile. Then, looking at the food, 'Actually, I think I'll pass on that, if you don't mind. I had a sandwich earlier and there's something about a hospital that seems to take away the appetite.'

'How is your husband?'

'Like most men, he's his own worst enemy, but he got treatment very fast. The doctor said he's been lucky and if he behaves himself he'll be home in a day or two.'

'And then your problems will really begin.' They exchanged a knowing look. Her grandfather had never been seriously ill but he could make a simple cold seem like double pneumonia. 'Could I make you a cup of tea, Mrs Saxon?'

'Hetty, please.' Then, 'Actually, what I really need is a bath and my bed. You must be tired too.' She patted her arm. 'Your room is on the right at the top of the stairs. It's not fancy, but it's comfortable and it has its own bathroom. There's plenty of hot water. Just make yourself at home, dear.'

People kept saying that to her, Annie thought, as Hetty, clearly exhausted by long hours at the hospital, took herself off to bed.

She smiled to herself as she got stuck into the dishes. This wasn't anything like being at home, but that was good. Just what she wanted, in fact. And she was happy to help, to be able to repay in some small way this unlooked for, unexpected kindness, hospitality.

And she could think while she was working.

The loss of Lydia's car had thrown her simple non-plan off the rails and now she needed a new one.

A new plan, a replacement car and a haircut, she decided, pushing her hair back from her face.

She should make a list, she thought, twitching her nose to keep the glasses in place.

Or maybe not.

Her life had been run by her diary secretary for years. A list of monthly, weekly, daily engagements had appeared on her desk, each month, week, morning without fail.

Everything organised down to the last minute. Even her escape had been meticulously planned. The how. The where. The when.

She'd still been doing things by the book until the wheels had come off. Literally.

At the time it had seemed like a disaster. Now it seemed like anything but. Hadn't kicking back, taking whatever life threw at her, been the whole point of this break from reality? Cooking and washing up hadn't figured on any list of things to do, but it certainly came under the heading of 'different'.

George hadn't reappeared by the time she'd finished, put the dishes away, wiped everything down, so, remembering his aversion to instant coffee, she made a pot of tea and then ventured into the main part of the house to find him.

The front hall had that shabby, comfortable look that old houses, occupied by the same family over generations, seemed to acquire. It was large, square, the polished floor covered by an old Turkish rug. There was a scarred oak table along one wall, piled with mail that had been picked up from the mat and left in a heap. Above it hung a painting of an open-topped vintage car, bonnet strapped down, numbered for a race, a leather-helmeted driver at the wheel.

A small brass plate on the frame read: 'George Saxon, 1928'. It was full of life, energy, glamour and she could see how it might have caught the imagination of a teenage girl in much the same way as photographs of her mother working at a clinic in an African village had inspired her to follow in her footsteps.

Despite George's misgivings, she hoped Xandra was more successful in achieving her dreams.

The living room door stood ajar but George wasn't there. The next door opened to reveal the dining room and, after tapping lightly on the remaining door, she opened it.

The study was a man's room. Dark colours, leather furniture.

There was an open Partner's desk against one wall, but George was sitting in a large leather wing chair pulled up to the fireplace, head resting against one of the wings, long legs propped on a highly polished brass fender, cellphone held loosely in his hand, eyes closed.

Fast asleep.

'George?' she murmured.

He didn't stir but the soft cashmere of his sweater was warm to the touch and she left her hand on his broad shoulder long after it became obvious that he wasn't going to wake without more vigorous intervention.

Eventually, though, she took it away, eased the phone from his long fingers and put it, carefully, on the table, then stood watching him for a moment, wondering whether to try harder to rouse him.

He looked exhausted and, instead, she reached out as if to smooth the strain lines from his face. But the intimacy of such a gesture made it unthinkable and she curled her fingers into her palms before they quite touched his skin.

She wouldn't have done that to a man she'd

known for years and George Saxon was practically
a stranger.

But then that was the difference.

He didn't know who she was. Didn't feel the
need to treat her with kid gloves. He'd kissed her
because something in her face had told him that was
what she wanted, and he'd been right. For the first
time in her adult life she didn't have to be guarded,
careful about how everything she said, did, would
be interpreted. Didn't have to worry about reading
'all about it' in the morning paper.

The sheer dizzying freedom of that hit her in a
rush and she knelt at his feet, uncurled her fingers
and let them rest lightly against his face.

Fingertips against the smooth skin at his temple,
palm against the exciting roughness of a day-old
beard. And then she leaned forward and touched her
lips to his.

Not a wake-up-and-kiss-me-back kiss, but a
promise to herself to be brave enough to embrace life,
embrace every new experience that offered itself.

To be wholly and completely herself.

He didn't stir and after a moment she leaned back
on her heels, then, leaving him to sleep, stood up
and let herself quietly out of the room before taking
the stairs that rose through the centre of the house.

She followed Hetty's directions and opened the
first door on the right. Her bag was at the foot of an
ornate wrought iron bed and, reassured that she was

in the right room, she switched on the light and closed the door.

The house was old and the room was large, with high ceilings. The en suite bathroom, a more recent addition, had taken a bite out of the room and the bed was tucked into the larger section of the remaining L.

The walls were decorated with old-fashioned flower-strewn wallpaper that went perfectly with the bed, the patchwork comforter, the dark oak antique furniture. The velvet button-back nursing chair, oval cheval mirror.

A moss-green rug that matched the velvet curtains lay in front of a dresser on the wide oak boards and she drew them to shut out the winter dark before taking a look at the bathroom.

The huge roll-top claw-footed bath with its brass fittings was, like everything else in the house, gleaming with care.

She turned on the taps and then, leaving the water to run, returned to the bedroom to open her bag, see what Lydia had packed for her.

She'd sent her a cheque to cover the basics. Underwear, a nightdress, toiletries. Just enough to see her through until she could buy what she needed. There was a pink T-shirt nightie, plain white underwear, a couple of brushed cotton shirts, socks.

Basic as you like, she thought with a smile. Perfect.

But, when it came to toiletries, the clean, simple

lines of the packaging disguised a world of luxury and she clutched the bag to her, hoping that her lookalike would get as much pleasure from the special treats she'd packed for her.

Smiling, she picked up a towel from a pile on the chair and then returned to the bathroom.

She uncapped a bottle and poured a little oil into the bath and the scent of lime blossom rose with the steam, enveloping her as she stripped off, piling up the cash she'd stowed about her body.

Not just the thousand pounds in her bra, but the rest of her running-away money that, on Lydia's insistence—who seemed to believe she'd be mugged the minute she stepped outside the hotel—she'd tucked around her waist inside her tights. Fortunately, Lydia hadn't felt the need to lose weight to keep the likeness true, so there had been ample room in the baggy jeans she'd been wearing.

Bearing in mind George's reaction to the thousand pounds she'd produced, it was probably a good thing that it had been safely out of reach, she thought as she sank beneath the water and closed her eyes, letting the warmth seep into her bones.

He'd been suspicious enough as it was. If she'd let him see just how much she was carrying on her, he would have called the police on the spot. Unless she'd owned up to her real identity, she'd be languishing in a police cell right now, up to her neck in hot water, instead of lying back in this deliciously scented bath.

Her mind drifted to the image of how she'd left him, dark head resting against the leather wing of his chair. The unfamiliar feel of the day-old beard shadowing his chin.

Her smile faded into a sigh of longing as she wondered how it would feel against her cheek, her neck, the delicate skin of her breast.

George stirred, opened his eyes, for a moment not sure where he was, only that something had disturbed him. A touch, a faint familiar scent. Then, as he focused on the paper and wood laid in the grate, waiting only for a match to bring the fire blazing into life, it all came flooding back. Where he was. And all the rest.

His father was in hospital.

His daughter had been suspended from the school he'd chosen with such care—a place apart from the pressures of family, where she could be whoever she wanted to be.

And the scent belonged to Annie Rowland, a woman with lips like the promise of spring who was on the run from something. Someone.

He was three times in trouble, he decided as he raised his hand to his own lips, wiping the back of it hard across them as if he could erase the disturbing thought that while he'd been sleeping Annie had been there. Had kissed him.

He shook his head. That had to be a figment of his imagination.

And yet the image of her kneeling at his feet was so vivid that he stood up abruptly, bumping against the table, sending a mug flying.

He made a grab for it, swearing as hot liquid slopped over the rim, scalding his fingers. Proof that someone had been there in the last minute or two. Someone who wouldn't have left him sleeping in a chair, but would have put her hand on his shoulder. Brushed her fingers across his cheek.

And, if he'd woken, would he have tumbled her in his lap, taken up where they'd left off? Finished what he'd so nearly started earlier that evening when he'd slipped the fake glasses on her nose? When he'd kissed her, wanting her to know that he wasn't fooled by her disguise, that he'd caught her out, only to discover himself snared by a woman who, just hours earlier, he'd dismissed as not worth a second glance.

Kidding himself.

Not that her first impression of him would have been particularly flattering. He'd been sarcastic, angry, torn. Wanting to be anywhere else in the world. Wanting only to be here.

And yet there had been something. A recognition, a dangerous edge, a challenge that had sparked between them from the moment she'd cannoned into his arms, fitting the empty space like a hand coming into a glove.

Damn Xandra for getting him involved, he

thought as he carried the mug through to the kitchen and grabbed his jacket from the hook. A woman was a complication he could do without right now. Any woman.

This one…

He caught his breath as he stepped outside. It was already close to freezing and his breath condensed and glowed in the concealed lights that lit the path to the gate and in the security lights that floodlit the garage. But he didn't hurry.

Cold air was exactly what he needed to clear his head and he took his time about checking that everything was safely locked, the alarms switched on before he fetched his holdall from his car.

He did the same inside, checking windows, sliding home bolts, setting the alarm, yawning as the warmth of the house stole over him.

He'd been fighting off sleep for hours, but it was long past time to surrender and, as he pushed open the bedroom door, he kicked off his shoes, pulled his shirt and sweater over his head in one move as he reached the bed, clicked on the bedside light.

And saw Annie's bag open at his feet.

What on earth…?

He straightened, half expecting to see her staring up at him from the pillow. But there was only a ridiculously girlish nightdress—pink with a cartoon rabbit that was saying 'Give me a hug'—that she'd thrown on the bed.

On his bed…

And then it hit him.

His mother had walked into her kitchen and found Annie preparing dinner and she'd leapt to the obvious conclusion that she was with him.

That they were an item. Together. Partners. All those ridiculous expressions used these days to describe a couple who were living together without the blessing of church or state.

He stooped to pick up his shirt and sweater, get out of there, but as he straightened he heard the door open behind him and there she was, reflected in the tall cheval mirror, with only a bath towel wrapped around her like a sarong, her arms full of the clothes she'd been wearing.

She dropped her clothes on the chair. Then, catching sight of her reflection, she pulled a face as she lifted her hands to her hair, using her fingers to push the damp strands off her face, tucking it first behind her ears, then pulling it forward, turning her head first one way, then the other, as if trying to decide what kind of style might suit her.

He'd been given a close-up of that fine bone structure earlier but now, without the distraction of badly cut hair, ugly glasses, he knew without doubt that it was a face he'd seen before.

But where?

Tall, skinny, bones that a camera would love, she had to be a model, he decided, but he didn't have time to think about it. Half hidden in the L, she hadn't seen him and, as she pulled free the tail of a towel that she'd tucked between her breasts, he said, 'I wouldn't do that…'

Practically leaping out of her skin, Annie spun round and her mouth went dry.

George Saxon, wrapped up in a soft shirt and cashmere sweater was a man to turn a woman's head. Now, stripped to the waist, his wide golden shoulders and chest were as bone-meltingly beautiful as a fine Greek bronze.

She swallowed. Managed to croak out, 'Your mother said…' before, realising exactly what his mother must have thought, the words died on her lips and she clutched her towel to her breast as she felt herself blush pink from head to toe. 'Oh…'

George watched, fascinated, as a wave of delicate pink enveloped Annie, not just her face, but her smooth, creamy neck and shoulders, to disappear beneath the towel she was clutching to her breast as she quickly cottoned onto exactly what the mix-up had been.

He knew he shouldn't think about that, but whatever she'd used in her bath smelled as inviting as the promise of a warm spring day and the temptation to unwrap her, see just how far that blush had gone, was almost irresistible.

'Oh, indeed,' he replied, his voice thick, his attempt at briskness failing miserably. 'It's entirely my fault,' he said, trying again. 'I should have explained.'

'She had more important things on her mind.'

'Yes.' Then, 'It's not a problem,' he said, moving to pick up his shoes, but Annie reached out and, with her hand on his arm, stopped him.

'Please. Don't go.'

He barely registered what she said, instead staring at her left hand, white, perfectly manicured nails painted a deep shade of pink against the darker skin of his arm and, when he finally looked up, there were only two things moving in the room. His heart as it pounded against the wall of his chest and the slight rise and fall of Annie's breasts as she breathed a little too fast.

And, as her words finally registered, what had been a simple misunderstanding seemed to become something more. Something that was meant.

One move, that was all it would take, and if she was looking for a night of forgetfulness in a stranger's arms, he would have said he was her man.

But, deep in his bones, he knew that, despite the disguise, the deception, Annie was not a one-night-stand kind of woman. He, on the other hand, had never been interested in anything else and, taking her hand in his, he held it for a moment, wanting her to know that he wasn't rejecting her but being a friend and discovered that she was trembling.

'What are you running from?'

Unable to speak, she shook her head and, swearing beneath his breath, he put his arm around her, pulled her against him.

'It'll be all right,' he said, holding her close, intensely aware of her breath against his naked chest. Her skin, warm and scented from the bath, against his.

Meaningless words, but they were all he could think of and, far from steady himself as she looked up at him, he stroked the dark smudge under one of her eyes with the pad of his thumb as if he could wipe the shadow away. Make everything better.

'You'll be safe here.'

Her response was no more than a murmur that whispered across his skin and he had to tear himself away from the temptation to go with the moment.

'Sleep well, Annie,' he said and, dropping a kiss on her poor tortured hair, he stepped back, grabbed his shoes and walked swiftly from the room. Closing the door firmly behind him with a snap before he changed his mind.

CHAPTER SEVEN

ANNIE stared at the closed door. 'I don't want to be safe!' she repeated, louder this time.

All her life she'd been kept safe by a grandfather afraid that he'd lose her, as he'd lost his son. She'd been educated at home by tutors, had very few friends—mothers tended to be nervous about inviting her to play when she arrived with a bodyguard in tow.

And it hadn't got any better as she got older. The only men her grandfather had allowed within touching distance had known better than to take liberties with the nation's sweetheart. And somehow she'd never managed to get beyond that.

She'd been so sure that George was different.

He'd run out on the family business, had at least one ex-wife, a broken relationship with his teenage daughter. She should have been able to rely on a man with a record like that to take advantage of a damsel in distress.

It wasn't as if she'd screamed when she found

him in her bedroom. On the contrary, when she'd turned and seen him she'd known exactly why women lost their heads over totally unsuitable men. Had been more than ready to lose hers. In every sense of the word.

Instead, after a promising start and despite the fact that she was a towel drop away from being naked, he'd kissed her on the top of the head as if she was six years old instead of twenty-six.

How lowering was that?

She looked at the hand with which she'd detained him, used it to tug free the towel, standing defiantly naked. Then, catching sight of herself in the mirror—all skin and bones—she didn't blame him. Who on earth would fall in lust with that? she thought, quickly pulling on the pink nightie to cover herself up.

Pink, cute. With a bunny on the front. Just about perfect for a six-year-old, she thought as she climbed into bed.

Or the oldest virgin in the country.

George woke from a dream in which a large, pink, girl rabbit wearing glasses had him pinned down to the bed, furry paws planted firmly on his chest.

Her familiar blue eyes appealed to him to save her while she murmured softly, over and over, 'I don't want to be safe…' And he knew that in some way they were, for her, one and the same thing.

He sat up with a start, certain that he'd seen those eyes somewhere before. Then he scrubbed his hands over his face to wake himself up properly, telling himself that he'd misheard her. She couldn't possibly have said what he thought she'd said.

It was still pitch dark outside, barely five o'clock, but he swung his legs over the narrow single bed of his boyhood room, not prepared to risk going back to sleep just in case the bunny was still there, lying in wait in his subconscious.

He dressed quickly and, very quietly so as not to disturb anyone, went downstairs and let himself out of the house.

Hetty glanced up from the kitchen scales where she was carefully weighing out flour as Annie walked into the kitchen.

'I'm so sorry,' she apologised. 'I had no idea it was so late.'

As she'd lain alone in the large comfortable bed, certain that once again sleep would elude her, she'd started to make a shopping list in her head. The first thing she was going to buy, she'd decided, was a slinky, sexy nightdress. The kind made for taking off rather than putting on. The last thing she remembered was trying to decide whether it should be black or red.

'I can't remember the last time I slept like that.'

'Well, you must have been tired after your journey. Can you make yourself breakfast? There are plenty of eggs, bacon…' She made a broad gesture at the collection of ingredients stacked on the kitchen table. 'I find cooking takes my mind off things.'

'A slice of toast will do me,' Annie said. 'And some tea. Can I make a cup for you?'

She smiled. 'That would be lovely. Thank you, dear.'

Annie dropped a couple of slices of bread into the toaster, put on the kettle.

'It's so quiet here,' she said.

'This used to be a farm. Didn't George tell you?' She looked up. 'How did you meet?'

'Actually, Hetty, George and I aren't…' she made a gesture that she hoped would cover the situation '…together.' She swallowed as George's mother, reaching for a bag of sugar, paused, a frown creasing her brow. 'My car broke down yesterday evening and I called the nearest garage. He came and picked me up.'

'George took out the tow-truck?' she asked, astonished.

'Not with any enthusiasm,' she admitted. 'I was going to call a cab to take me to the motel but Xandra asked me to stay.'

'Xandra?' She raised her hand to her mouth. 'You mean…? But I…'

'It's all right. An easy mistake to make and George

was the complete gentleman…' unfortunately '…and retired, leaving me in sole possession of the bedroom. I do hope he wasn't too uncomfortable.'

'He probably used his old bedroom,' she said, pouring the sugar into the scales. 'Pity. It's about time he settled down with a decent woman.'

'I'm sure he'd be much happier with an indecent one.'

His mother laughed. 'No doubt. Maybe that's why he was in such a bad mood when I took him out some tea earlier. I sent Xandra on an errand to keep her out of his way.'

'Oh. I had assumed she was with him. She seems very keen.'

'I know. My husband dotes on her. Let's her do anything she wants.' She sighed. 'Life would have been a great deal easier if George had been a girl. He wouldn't have been so hard. Expected so much…' Hetty sighed, then smiled as Annie handed her a cup of tea. 'Even so, he really shouldn't have let her get so involved with the garage.'

'She would never have stuck at it unless she really wanted to be a motor mechanic,' she said, buttering the toast.

'George told you about that?'

'No, it was Xandra. She's very determined. And I should warn you that she doesn't want to go back to boarding school. She wants to stay here.'

'She already spends most of her holidays with

us. Her mother has other interests. Pass me that bowl, will you?'

Annie would have liked to ask about George. What interests kept him away? But that would be invading his privacy and, instead, she handed Hetty a large old-fashioned crockery mixing bowl.

'Are you making a Christmas cake?'

'It's silly really. You can buy such good ones and I don't suppose George—my George—will be able to eat it. The doctor said he needs to lose some weight.'

'Walking is good. For the heart,' she added. Then, sucking melted butter from her thumb, 'Can I do anything to help?'

'You could make a start creaming the sugar and butter, if you like.' She tipped the sugar into the bowl, adding butter she'd already measured and chopped up. 'You'll find a wooden spoon in the drawer.'

There was no fancy electric mixer to make light work of it, but Annie had seen the process often enough as a child to know what she had to do.

'What's the problem with your car?' Hetty asked when she'd spooned the last of the spices into a saucer and everything was measured. 'Will it take long to fix?'

'It's terminal, I'm afraid. George is going to arrange for it to be crushed.'

'But that's—'

Before she could finish, Xandra burst through

the door. 'Got them! Oh, hi, Annie.' She dumped the box on one of the chairs. 'I've been up in the attic sorting out the Christmas decs. Now all we need is a tree.'

'Why don't you and Annie take the Land Rover and go and pick one up from the farm?' her grandmother suggested.

'That would be so brilliant.'

Annie blinked at the transformation from last night's moody teen to this childlike enthusiasm.

'But I…'

'What?'

'I really should be going.'

'Where? You're staying for the Christmas market, aren't you? Annie can stay for the weekend, can't she, Gran?'

'It's fine with me.'

'But you don't know me from Adam,' Annie protested. 'Besides, wouldn't you rather go to the farm with your father?'

'You mean the Grinch?'

'That's not fair, Xan,' Hetty said.

'Oh, please. He hates Christmas and we all know why.' Then, 'Come on, Annie, let's go and choose the biggest tree we can find.'

She swallowed. The scent of the newly cut evergreen brought indoors never failed to bring back that terrible Christmas when her parents hadn't come home.

'You will stay?' the girl pressed. 'We could go to the market together. It'll be fun.'

She looked up, ready to explain that she really had to move on, but Hetty, exhaustion in every line of her face, met her gaze with a silent plea that she couldn't ignore.

'Let's go and get the tree and we'll take it from there,' she said.

'Excellent. Can we go now, Gran?'

'I'll be glad to have the place to myself. Not too big,' she called after her, adding a silent, 'Thank you,' to Annie before raising her voice to add, 'We don't want a repeat of last year.' Then, 'Wrap up. It's cold out. There's a scarf on the hook. Gloves in the drawer.'

'What happened last year?' Annie asked Xandra, tucking the ends of her hair into the woolly hat before she hauled herself up behind the wheel of an elderly Land Rover.

'Granddad came home with a ten-foot tree and we couldn't get it through the door. He's really silly about Christmas.'

'Is he? You spend a lot of time with your grand-parents?'

She pulled a face. 'We used to have a lovely house with a garden, but my mother took an interior decorating course and caught minimalism, so traded it in for a loft apartment on the Melchester quays. Not the kind of place for a girl with engine oil under her fingernails.'

'There's such a thing as a nail brush,' she pointed out, biting back the *What about your father?* question.

'I suppose, but my mother treats Christmas as a design opportunity. Last year it was silver and white with mauve "accents".' She did the thing with her fingers to indicate the quotes.

'Mauve?' Annie repeated.

'With the tiniest, tiniest white lights.' And, putting on a clipped accent, Xandra said, 'All terribly, terribly tasteful, dahling.' Then, 'Christmas isn't supposed to be tasteful.'

'Isn't it?' Annie asked, sobering as she thought about the Dickens-inspired designer co-ordinated green, red and gold that traditionally decked the halls of King's Lacey for the festive season. 'What is it supposed to be?'

Xandra's response was a broad grin. 'Stick around and see what I've got planned.' Then, with a groan as she saw her father, 'Come on, let's get out of here.'

George had emerged from the workshop and was striding purposefully in their direction and by the time she'd managed to start the cold engine he was at the window and she had no choice but to push it open. He was wearing overalls and there was a smear of grease on his cheek that her fingers itched to wipe away before her lips planted a kiss in that exact spot.

Losing her mind, clearly, she decided, keeping her hands firmly on the steering wheel, her eyes firmly on him, managing a fairly coherent, 'Good morning.' Unable to resist saying, 'I hope you managed to sleep well.'

He lifted an eyebrow, acknowledging the reference to her turning him out of his bed.

'Well enough,' he replied, although he'd apparently had to think about it. 'You?'

'Like a log for the first time in as long as I can remember,' she said gratefully. 'Thank you.'

He nodded. 'You look…rested.' Then, as he wiped his hands on a rag, 'Where are you two off to?'

'We're going to the farm,' she said. 'To buy a tree.'

'Come on, Annie. Let's *go*,' Xandra butted in impatiently.

He put his hand on the open window to keep her where she was. 'Tree?' He frowned.

'A *Christmas* tree? You remember *Christmas*, don't you? Peace on earth, goodwill, tacky decs, bad songs. Terrible presents.'

His jaw tightened. 'I have heard of it.' Then, looking at Annie, 'Have you ever driven a four-wheel drive?'

About to assure him that, despite all evidence to the contrary, she'd not only been taught to drive everything on her grandfather's estate by an ex-police driving instructor, but had been trained in survival driving, she managed to stop herself.

And not simply because mentioning the fact that her grandfather owned an estate seemed like a bad idea.

'Why?' she asked innocently. 'Is it different to driving a car?'

'In other words, no,' he said, opening the door. 'Shift over, I'll take you.'

'Can't you just take me through it?' she suggested. 'I know how busy you are and I've put you to more than enough trouble.'

'You think?' He held her gaze for so long that she was afraid he knew exactly what she was doing. Then, shaking his head, 'It'll be quicker if I run you there.'

'I'm really sorry,' she said as she edged her bottom along the seat. 'It was your mother's idea and she's been so kind. It's the least I can do.'

Xandra was staring straight ahead, rigid with tension.

'Budge up,' she urged.

The girl moved no more than a hand's width and Annie could almost feel the waves of animosity coming off her. Clearly her plan to get father and daughter to bond over the purchase of a Christmas tree wasn't going to be as simple as she'd hoped.

That said, she was a little tense herself as George squashed in beside her, his arm brushing against her as he reached for the gearstick. He glanced at her, asking her with the slightest lift of his eyebrow if she was all right. She gave a barely discernible shrug to indicate that she was fine.

As if.

She was crushed up against the kind of man who would light up any woman's dreams, her cheek against his shoulder, her thigh trembling against the hard muscles of his leg. She could feel every move he made, every breath and even the familiar smell of hot oil from the engine of the aged vehicle couldn't mask the scent of warm male.

It was too noisy to talk but as they came to a halt at a busy roundabout he turned to her.

'You'll have more room if you put your arm on my shoulder,' he said, looking down at her. But for a moment, mesmerised by his sensuous lower lip, close enough to kiss, she didn't, couldn't, move. Then, before she could get a grip, ease her arm free and lay it across those wide shoulders, Xandra abruptly shifted sideways.

'I'm…fine,' she managed as she reluctantly eased herself away from his warmth.

The Christmas tree farm wasn't far and they were soon pulling off the road and into an area cleared for a car park.

Beside it was the seasonal shop in a little chalet decorated with fake snow and strings of fairy lights. In front of it there was a children's ride, a bright red sleigh with Rudolph—complete with flashing nose— and Santa, with his sack of parcels, at the reins.

As soon as they came to a halt, Xandra opened the door and leapt down, not waiting for her or her father, disappearing stiff-legged, stiff-necked into the plantation.

'Are you coming?' Annie paused on the edge of the seat, looking back as she realised that George hadn't moved.

'You know me,' he said, his face expressionless. 'I'm just the driver.'

'I'm sorry.'

'It's not your fault.'

'No. And I am truly grateful to you for stepping in. Xandra wants to decorate the house for your father before he comes home from the hospital.'

Or was it really for him? she wondered.

Despite everything she'd said, he'd said, was Xandra hoping that he'd relent over closing the garage, stay for the holiday? That they'd all have a perfect fairy-tale Christmas together, the kind that proper families had in story books?

Dickens, she thought as she jumped down, had a lot to answer for.

Hitting the uneven ground jarred the ankle she'd wrenched the day before and she gave a little yelp.

And then she moaned.

'What?' George asked.

'Nothing…' She let the word die away as she hung onto the door.

Muttering something that she was clearly not

meant to hear, he climbed out and walked round the Land Rover to see for himself.

'It's nothing,' she repeated, letting go of the door with one hand just long enough to wave him away. 'I gave my ankle a bit of a wrench yesterday when I stepped in that pothole and just now, well, the drop was further than I thought...' Enough. Don't overdo it, Annie, she told herself and taking a steadying breath, she straightened herself, touched her toe to the ground. Bravely fought back a wince. 'Give me a minute,' she said with a little gasp. 'I'll be fine.'

'Let me see.'

She didn't have to feign the gasp as he put his hands around her waist and lifted her back up onto the seat, then picked up her left foot, resting her ankle in the palm of his hand.

'It doesn't look swollen,' he said, gently feeling around the bone, the instep and he looked up, slate eyes suddenly filled with suspicion.

'No. I told you. It'll be fine.' She slid down, forcing him back, and began to limp after Xandra.

'Wait!'

'I promised Hetty I'd keep an eye on her,' she said, not looking back. 'Make sure she keeps her ambitions below ceiling height.'

'Oh, for heaven's sake,' he said, closing the door and coming after her. 'Here,' he said, taking her arms and putting them around his neck. She scarcely had time to react to his irritable command before he'd bent and picked her up. 'Hang on.'

He didn't need to tell her twice and she hung on for dear life, arms around his neck, cheek in the crook of his warm neck as he walked across to the wooden chalet, carried her up the steps and set her down on a chair.

'Stay there and try not to get into any more trouble,' he said, picking up her foot and turning another chair for it to rest on. 'Okay?' his said, his face level with hers.

'Okay,' she said a touch breathlessly.

He nodded. 'Right. I'd better go and make sure Xandra doesn't pick out something that would be more at home in Trafalgar Square.'

'Wait!' she said and, before he could straighten, took his chin in her hand as she searched her pockets for a tissue.

He must have shaved last night after he'd left her, she realised, feeling only the slight rasp of morning stubble against her palm as she reached up and gently wiped the grease off his cheek. Then, because he was looking at her in a way that made her insides melt, she said, 'George Saxon and Son has a reputation to maintain.'

She'd meant to sound brisk, businesslike, matter-of-fact but her voice, trained to deliver a speech to the back of a banqueting hall, for once refused to co-operate and it came out as little more than a whisper.

'And what about Annie Rowland?' he asked, his face expressionless.

'What? I haven't got grease on my face, have I?' she asked, instinctively touching the same place on her own cheek.

'Not grease,' he said, lifting her glasses off her nose and slipping them into the top pocket of his overalls. 'Something far worse.'

'Oh, but—'

He stopped her protest by planting a kiss very firmly on her lips. For a moment she tried to talk through it but then, as the warmth of his lips penetrated the outer chill, heating her through to the bone, a tiny shiver of pleasure rippled through her and she forgot what she was trying to say.

Instead, she clutched at his shoulder, closed her eyes and, oblivious to the woman sitting by the till, she kissed him back. Let slip a tiny mew of disappointment as he drew back and the cold rushed back in.

She opened her eyes and for a moment they just looked at each other before, without another word, he turned and walked out of the door.

The woman behind the counter cleared her throat as, slightly dazed, Annie watched George follow the path his daughter had taken between the trees.

'Are you all right?' she asked.

'I'm not sure,' she said, raising cold fingers to hot lips. 'I'm really not at all sure.'

'Only there are signs warning about the uneven paths,' she said defensively.

'Are there?' She watched George until he disappeared from sight and then turned to look at the woman.

'It says we're not responsible—'

'Oh!' Annie said, finally catching onto the fact that she wasn't referring to the hiccup in her heartbeat, her ragged pulse rate. Or the way George had stolen her glasses before kissing her.

The woman was only concerned about the fact that she'd apparently injured her ankle in their car park and might decide to sue the pants off them.

She shook her head. 'Don't worry about it. I hurt it yesterday,' she said, reassuring her. 'Today was no more than a reminder.'

'Well, that's a relief. You wouldn't believe...' She let it go, smiled, then followed her gaze as she looked along the path that George had taken. 'It's good your man is so caring.'

'Oh, but he isn't...'

Her man.

She'd only met him last night. Barely knew him. And he didn't know her at all. No one who knew her would dare to kiss her the way he'd kissed her.

And yet she'd been closer to him in that short time than almost any man she'd ever known. She already cared about him in ways she had only dreamed of. And his daughter.

She'd grown up without a father of her own and if she could heal the breach between them she would go home knowing that she'd done something good.

'Can I get you something while you're waiting? Tea? Coffee? Hot chocolate?'

The little wooden chalet was, it seemed, more than simply a place to pay for the trees, the bundles of mistletoe and holly stacked up outside.

There was a little counter for serving hot drinks, cakes and mince pies and the walls were lined with shelves displaying seasonal decorations made by local craftsmen, although she was the only customer for the moment, despite the cars lined up outside. Obviously everyone else was out in the plantation picking out their trees.

Annie ordered a mince pie and a cup of hot chocolate and then, while she was waiting, instead of ignoring the decorations as she usually did, she looked around her, hoping to find something that would amuse Xandra.

There were beautiful handmade candles, charming wooden decorations. All perfectly lovely. All so wonderfully…tasteful.

Outside, a child climbed in the sleigh alongside Santa. His mother put a coin in the machine and it began to move in a motion designed to make over-excited children sick, while it played *Rudolph the Red-Nosed Reindeer*.

Not tasteful at all.

'Here you are.' The woman brought her chocolate and mince pie. 'Would you like the paper?' she asked, offering her one of the red tops. 'Something to look at while you're waiting.'

About to refuse, she changed her mind, deciding to check out the kind of coverage she'd got yesterday. Make sure there was nothing that would rouse the slightest suspicion in an eagle-eyed editor or set alarms bells ringing if anyone in her own office took more than the usual cursory glance.

'Thanks. That would be great.'

A picture of Lydia leaving the Pink Ribbon Lunch had made the front page. With rumours of a wedding, that was inevitable, but the hat, a last-minute special from her favourite designer featuring a Pink Ribbon spangled veil, had successfully blurred her features.

She'd seen so many photographs of herself, her head at just that angle as she'd turned to smile for the cameras, that even she found it hard to believe that it wasn't actually her.

And if Lydia had a bloom that she'd been lacking in recent months, the caption writer had put his own spin on that.

Lady Rose was radiant as she left the Pink Ribbon Lunch yesterday before flying to Bab el Sama for a well-earned break before Christmas at King's Lacey, her family home. The question is, will she be on her own? See page five.

She turned to page five, where there was a double-page spread including a recent picture of her, smiling as she left some event with Rupert. Thankful it was over, no doubt.

There was a huge aerial photograph of Bab el Sama, and another distant shot of the beach taken from the sea, along with many words written by someone who had never been there—no one from the press had ever set foot in the place—speculating on the luxury, the seclusion of a resort that was, apparently, the perfect place for lovers.

Put together the words 'radiant' and 'lovers' and read between the lines…

Yuck.

But, then again, it was only what she'd expected and with luck the possibility would keep the paparazzi fixed to the spot, hoping for a picture that would earn them a fortune.

She smiled. Sorry, chaps, she thought, as she closed the paper, folded it over so that the front page was hidden and put it back on the counter. Then, brimful of goodwill despite rather than because of the season, she said, 'I don't suppose I could persuade you to part with Rudolph, could I?'

'You'd be surprised how many people have asked me that,' she said, 'but we've only got him on hire during December.'

'Pity.'

'Believe me,' she said as the child demanded another ride and the song started up again, 'after the first hundred times, it feels like a lifetime.'

CHAPTER EIGHT

GEORGE followed his daughter down the path to the area where the farmer and his son were harvesting the trees.

The boy, seventeen or eighteen, brawny, good-looking, smiled as he looked up and caught sight of Xandra.

'Can I help?' he asked.

'I need a tree,' she said, with the cool, assessing look that women had been giving men since Adam encountered Eve in the Garden of Eden. 'A big one,' she added, turning away to inspect trees that had already been dug up and netted.

It was a move calculated to draw the boy closer and he followed as if on a string. It was like watching the rerun of an old movie, he thought. She was younger than her mother had been when she'd looked at him like that, but she already had the moves down pat.

'With roots or without?' the boy asked.

'Without,' he replied for her, stepping forward to make his presence felt.

'With,' Xandra countered, not even bothering to look at him. 'I want to plant it in the garden after Christmas.'

'Okay. If you'd like to choose one I'll dig it up for you.'

'What's wrong with those?' George said, nodding at the trees that were ready to go.

'I want to choose my own,' Xandra said.

'And it's best to get it as fresh as possible,' the boy added. Wanting to flex his muscles for a pretty girl. 'I'll get a decent root ball with it and wrap it in sacking for you. That'll give it a better chance.'

'Thanks,' she said before turning, finally, to acknowledge his presence. 'Where's Annie?' she asked, realising that he was on his own.

'She hurt her ankle getting out of the Land Rover. I left her in the shop with her foot up.' Then, in an effort to move things along, he indicated a nicely shaped tree and said, 'What about that one?'

'It's not tall enough.'

Clearly whichever tree he'd chosen was going to be rejected but he pressed on. 'It'll be at least two feet taller once it's out of the ground and in a pot.'

He looked at the boy, who was smart enough to agree with him. 'It's a lovely tree,' he added, but if he hoped to curry favour he was talking to the wrong man. He'd been eighteen once, and this was his daughter.

Xandra shrugged. 'Okay. But I want one for outside as well. A really *big* one.'

About to ask her who was going to put it up, he stopped himself, aware that the boy, if he had anything about him, would leap in with an offer to do it for her.

She'd had sixteen years without him to put up a tree for her. Maybe one really big one would make a bit of a dent in the overdraft.

'No more than ten feet from the ground,' he told the boy and, when she would have objected, 'I won't be able to carry anything bigger than that on the roof of the Land Rover.' Even that would be a push.

Then, beating down the urge to grab her by the arm, drag her back to the shop where he could keep her within sight, he said, 'Don't take too long about choosing it. I want to get Annie back into the warm,' he said, turning to go back to her.

'Is she badly hurt?' She sounded concerned.

'She's putting a brave face on it,' he said, rubbing the flat of his palm over his jaw, where he could still feel the warm touch of her fingers, despite the chill.

It had been the same last night. After leaving her he'd taken a shower, shaved, anything to distance himself from the touch of her hand that had burned like a brand on his arm. Somehow he doubted that even a cold shower would have saved him from the pink bunny.

Now he'd kissed her again, just to shut her up for a moment, he told himself, but this time she'd kissed him back. Yet still he was left with the extraordinary sense that for her it was all brand-new.

How crazy was that? She had to be in her mid-twenties at least.

Xandra hesitated, but only for a moment, before turning to the boy. 'Okay, I'm going to trust you to choose the big tree—'

'I know just the one,' he said eagerly. 'A real beauty. You'll love it.' And Xandra bestowed a gracious smile on him before, just a touch of colour darkening her cheekbones, she quickly turned away and swept off up the path.

For a moment they both stood and watched her, each lost for a moment in his own thoughts.

The boy was only seeing Christmas coming early.

His thoughts were darker as he remembered the moment when, not much older than the youth at his side, she'd been put in his arms, the realisation that she was his little girl. The shattering need to protect her. Make her life perfect.

Remembering the beautiful little girl with dark curls who'd run not to him, but to his father for hugs. Who had called Penny's second husband— living in the house he'd paid for—'daddy'.

* * *

Annie looked up as he followed Xandra into the chalet.

'Did you find what you were looking for?' she asked, her eyes narrowing as she looked at him.

'I think I can safely guarantee that our trees will be the best that money can buy.'

She still had her left foot propped up and, ignoring the empty chairs, he picked it up, sat down and placed it on his knee, leaving his hand on the curve between ankle and foot.

It was a slender foot, a slender ankle and there wasn't the slightest sign of a swelling.

'Trees?' she asked.

'A six-footer for inside the house. Something rather more stately for outside.'

'Oh, trees *plural*. You're going to need a ton of tinsel, Xandra,' she said, watching her as she wandered around the shop, checking out what they had to offer.

'I'm working on it,' she said, picking up one of the decorations, then putting it back.

'How's your ankle?' George asked, reclaiming Annie's attention.

'Fine, really,' she assured him, not quite meeting his gaze, adding to his certainty that she had faked the injury. But why?

Could it be that she saw the garage as a sanctuary? Wanted to stay on?

'It was nothing that hot chocolate and a mince pie

couldn't cure,' she assured him, making a move to put it down, but he kept his hand firmly in place.

'Best to keep it up for as long as possible,' he said.

She took her time about answering him, dabbing at the crumbs on the plate in front of her and sucking them off her finger before, finally, lifting her lashes with a look that went straight to his gut.

Was it deliberate? Did she know what she was doing?

Usually, when he looked at a woman, when she looked back, they both knew exactly what they wanted, but Annie wasn't like any woman he'd ever met.

She left him floundering.

'So,' he said quickly, glad he was wearing loose overalls over his trousers so that she couldn't see the disturbing effect she had on him, 'what's your plan for today?'

Her lips parted over perfect teeth but, before she could tell him, Xandra said, 'She's staying with us until after the weekend. Gran asked her,' she added, glaring at him, daring him to offer an argument.

But if his mother had already asked her to stay, why would she—?

Oh. Right.

She'd seen an opportunity to throw him and Xandra together and, instead of seizing the moment, he'd gone in with both feet and made a complete cobblers of it.

'Not that she'd be able to go gallivanting all over the place sightseeing with a dodgy ankle,' she added.

'Honestly,' Annie said, looking at him, her eyes offering him her assurance that if he was unhappy she'd make her excuses and leave, 'it's not that bad.'

'Best not take any chances,' he said, attempting to unravel the curious mixture of elation and dismay he felt at the prospect of her staying on for several more days.

Relief that she wasn't going to walk away, disappear. That he'd never know what happened to her. Who she really was.

Dismay because he wanted to protect her from whatever was out there, threatening her. And that unnerved him.

'I'm having some water,' Xandra said, examining the contents of a glass-fronted fridge. She turned to him. 'Do you want anything?'

To be back at his beach house with nothing on his mind more important than the design of a multi-million-pound software program, a mild flirtation with a pretty woman, he thought, as he reached for his wallet. One with curves and curls and an uncomplicated smile that let you know exactly what was on her mind.

Since that wasn't an option, he said, 'Coffee and—'

'I don't need your money,' she snapped as he offered her a note. Then, perhaps remembering where the money in her own purse had come from, quickly said, 'Black with too much sugar, right?'

'Thanks.'

He'd been about to tell her to buy the angel she'd looked at, but decided against it. She wasn't a little girl he could buy with a doll.

'And?' she added. He must have looked puzzled because she said, 'You said "and".'

'And if you could run to a couple of those mince pies,' he said, 'it would fill a gap. I seem to have missed breakfast.'

'Sugar, fat and caffeine?' She shook her head. 'Tut, tut, tut.' But she turned to the woman behind the counter and said, 'The water for me, a heart attack for George... And what's that, Annie? Hot chocolate? Do you want a top-up?'

'No, I'm good, thanks.'

'Hot chocolate and a mince pie? Have a care, Annie,' he warned her with a grin. 'The food police will be after you too.'

'At least I had a slice of toast before I left the house this morning.'

'Buttered, of course. My father isn't a man to have anything as new-fangled as low-fat spread in the house.'

'Buttered,' she admitted, smiling as she conceded the point. 'But it was unsalted butter.'

'Honestly. What are you two like?' Xandra said disapprovingly. 'You're supposed to be mature adults. I'd get the "breakfast is the most important meal of the day" lecture if I ate like that.'

'Not from me,' he assured her.

'Well, no. Obviously. You'd have to be there.'

'I was,' he reminded her. 'Out of interest, what did you have for breakfast?'

'Gran made us both porridge. I sliced an apple over mine and added a drizzle of maple syrup.'

'Organic, of course.'

'Of course.'

'Well, good for you.' Annie, he noticed, lips pressed together to keep a smile in check, was being very careful to avoid eye contact, this time for all the right reasons. 'Actually,' he continued, 'you seem to have overlooked the fact that there's fruit in the mincemeat.'

Xandra snorted, unimpressed, but she turned away quickly. He was hoping it was so that he wouldn't see that, like Annie, she was trying not to laugh.

He was probably fooling himself, he thought, reaching for the paper lying on the counter to distract himself with the sports headlines on the back page so he wouldn't dwell on how much that hurt.

'Here you are.' Xandra put his coffee and pastries in front of him, then, sipping from the bottle she was holding, wandered over to the window to watch for the arrival of the trees. Or possibly the young man who'd be bringing them.

'It'll take him a while to dig up two big trees,' he warned her.

'Well, I'm sorry to take up so much of your time.' She took the paper from him, pulled out a chair and turned it over and, having glanced at the front page, opened it up. She was using it as a barrier rather than because she was interested in world news, he thought, but after a moment she looked up, stared at Annie, then looked at the paper again.

'Has anyone ever told you how much you look like Lady Rose, Annie?' she asked.

'Who?' she asked, reaching for the paper, but he beat her to it.

'You know.' She made a pair of those irritating quote marks with her fingers. 'The "people's virgin".'

'*Who?*' he asked.

Xandra leaned over and pointed to a picture of a man and a woman. 'Lady Rose Napier. The nation's sweetheart. She came to Dower House a couple of years ago for prize-giving day. Chauffeur, body-guards, the Warthog genuflecting all over the place.'

Since George paid the school fees, he received invitations to all school events as a matter of courtesy. Did his best to make all of them.

'I must have missed that one,' he said, realising that Lady Rose was the pampered 'princess' whose wedding plans were the talk of the tabloids.

He looked up from the paper to check the likeness for himself. 'Xandra's right,' he said. 'You do look like her.' Which perhaps explained why she'd seemed vaguely familiar.

'I wish,' Annie said with a slightly shaky laugh. 'I was just reading about her. She's holed up in luxurious seclusion in a palace owned by the Ramal Hamrahn royal family. I could do with some of that.'

'According to this, she's with that old bloke she's going to marry.' Xandra pulled a face. 'I'd rather stay a virgin.'

'I'd rather you did too,' George said.

She glanced at him. 'You're a fine one to talk.'

'Your mother was eighteen,' he protested, then stopped. This was not a conversation he wanted to have with his sixteen-year-old daughter. 'Did you meet her? Lady Rose?'

'In other words, did I win a prize? Sorry, they don't give one for car maintenance.' Then, since that didn't get the intended laugh, 'Lady Rose is nearly as old as Annie. I suppose she must be getting desperate.'

He looked at the picture of the man beside her. 'He's not that old,' he protested.

'He's thirty-nine. It says so right there.'

With his own thirty-sixth birthday in sight, that didn't seem old to him, but when he'd been sixteen it would probably have seemed ancient.

'It also says he's rich. Owns a castle in Scotland,

estates in Norfolk and Somerset and is heir to an earldom.'

'I think that cancels out "old",' he countered, looking up from the photograph of the two of them leaving some function together to compare her with Annie.

If you ignored the clothes, the woolly hat pulled down to hide not just her hair but most of her forehead, the likeness was striking.

And Annie had admitted to cutting her hair, borrowing the clothes she was wearing. She'd even talked about security men watching her night and day.

If the evidence that she'd flown to some place called Bab el Sama hadn't been right in front of him, it might have crossed his mind that Annie was Lady Rose Napier.

Assuming, of course, that she really had gone there. But why wouldn't she? It was the ultimate getaway destination. Luxury, privacy.

Why would she swap that for this?

'Rich, smitch,' Xandra said dismissively. 'Lady Rose doesn't need the money. Her father was the Marquess of St Ives and he left her a fortune. And her grandfather is a duke.'

'How do you know all this?'

'Everything she does is news. She's the virgin princess with a heart of gold. An example to us all.'

She clutched at her throat to mime throwing up.

'I'd have thought a woman like that would be fighting off suitors.'

'Yes, well, she's been surrounded by bodyguards all her life, has a posse of photographers in her face wherever she goes and she has a whiter than white image to maintain. She can never let her hair down, kick off and have fun like everyone else, can she?' She thought about it for a moment. 'Actually, you've got to feel just a bit sorry for her.'

'Have you?' he asked, thinking about the way Annie had reached out to him last night. Her whispered 'I don't want to be safe'. 'What about you, Annie?'

'Do I feel sorry for her?' she asked, looking at the picture.

That was what he'd meant, but there was something about the way she was avoiding his eyes that bothered him.

'Would you marry the old guy in the picture?' he pressed.

She looked up then. Straight, direct. 'Not unless I was in love with him.'

'Oh, puh-lease,' Xandra said. Then, taking back the paper, she compared the two pictures and shrugged. 'Maybe she is in love. There was a rumour going around that she was anorexic, but she looks a lot better here. It's a pity, really.'

'What is?' he asked, never taking his eyes off Annie.

It all fitted, he thought.

The timing was right. The poise. He'd even thought that she was acting as if she were royalty when she'd left him to close the tow-truck door behind her. He doubted that Lady Rose Napier, with a chauffeur and bodyguards in attendance, had ever had to do that in her life.

But it had to be coincidence. There was a likeness, it was true, but wasn't everyone supposed to have a double somewhere? And why on earth would a woman with a fortune at her command take off in a rattle bucket car when she could be going first-class all the way to paradise with Mr Big?

'What's a pity?' he repeated sharply.

Xandra gave an awkward little shrug, shook her head, clearly embarrassed, which had to be a first.

'Nothing. It's just that in the earlier picture the likeness is more pronounced.'

When she was thinner? A little less attractive? Was that what his tactless daughter had stopped herself from saying?

'But if Annie worked at it a bit, grew her hair, had the right clothes, make-up, I bet one of those lookalike agencies would snap her up.'

Annie opened her mouth, presumably to protest, but Xandra wasn't finished.

'You'd have to wear high heels,' she went on, getting carried away in her enthusiasm. 'She's really tall. But I bet that if you put on a pound or two you could do it.'

'What about the eyes?' George said, trying to see her not in baggy jeans, a chain store fleece jacket with a woolly hat pulled down to cover her hair, but a designer gown cut low to reveal creamy shoulders, long hair swept up. Her face transformed with make-up. Jewels at her throat. He seemed to get stuck on the shoulders… 'Aren't they the big give-away?'

'What?' she said, her attention shifting to the sound of a tractor pulling into the car park. She dropped the paper, more interested in what was happening outside. 'Oh, that's not a problem. She could use contacts.'

'Of course she could,' he said, his own attention focused firmly on the woman sitting on the far side of the table. 'So does that appeal as a career move?'

The corner of Annie's mouth lifted in a wry smile. 'You mean if I were a little younger, a little taller, wore a wig, contacts and plenty of make-up?'

'And if you put on a few pounds,' he reminded her. A little weight to fill out the hollows beneath her collarbone. Hollows that matched those of Lady Rose Napier in her evening gown.

'Much more of your mother's meat pie and buttered toast and that won't be a problem,' she replied, the smile a little deeper, but still wry.

'As good a reason to stay as any other,' he suggested. 'As long as you remember to add garlic to the mash.'

'Are you suggesting that I'm scrawny?'

'The trees are here, George.' His daughter impatiently demanded his attention and he pushed back his chair, got to his feet, never taking his eyes off Annie.

'Not if I have any sense,' he replied. 'And you can save the expense of contact lenses. Your eye colour is more than a match for the people's virgin.'

He took her glasses from his pocket and, taking her hand, placed them in her palm, closing her fingers over them, holding them in place as he was held by Annie's vivid gaze.

'They look an awful lot bigger on the trailer than they did growing,' Xandra said, breaking the spell. 'Will they be safe on the roof?'

'Don't worry about it,' he said, telling himself that he was glad of the distraction. 'If it's going to be a problem I'm sure your lovelorn swain will be happy to offer a personal delivery service.'

'My what? Oh, for goodness' sake,' she said, rolling her eyes at him before stomping down the steps and striding across the car park.

'I'd better go and find some rope,' he said, still not moving.

'Is there anything I can do to help?' Annie asked, the glasses still clutched in her hand.

'I think you've done more than enough for one

day, Annie. If you don't fancy lookalike work, you could always take up acting.'

'Acting?'

He noted the nervous swallow, the heightened colour that flushed across her cheekbones with relief. Despite his earlier suspicion that she might be a practised con woman, it was clear that, whatever she was hiding, she wasn't a practised liar.

'I don't understand.'

'There's nothing wrong with your ankle,' he said bluntly.

'Oh.' The colour deepened. 'How did you guess?'

'I've rarely encountered one in less perfect condition,' he said, reliving the feel of it beneath his palm. 'In fact, I'm seriously hoping that you'll take Xandra's advice to heart about wearing high heels.'

'I didn't pack any.'

'No? Well, you can't run in high heels, can you?'

'If you hadn't gone all macho over the car—'

'Oh, right. Blame the sucker.'

'It wasn't like that,' she protested. 'I just thought—'

'I know what you thought,' he said curtly, before she could say the words out loud. Determined to crush any foolish notion that throwing him into close proximity with Xandra would produce a cosy father-daughter bond. 'I have no doubt you imagined you were helping, but some relationships can't be fixed.'

No matter how much you might regret that.

'Not without putting a little effort into it,' she came right back at him, her eyes flashing with more than a touch of anger as if he'd lit some personal touchpaper. The air seemed to fizzle with it and he wondered what would have happened if, instead of listening to his head last night and walking away, he'd listened to her.

'I don't want to be safe...'

He took a step back, needing to put some space between them, but she wasn't done.

'Don't give up on her, George,' she said, leaning towards him, appealing to him. 'Don't give up on yourself.'

'I'm sure you mean well, Annie, but don't waste your time playing Santa Claus. It's not going to happen.' He pushed the paper towards her. 'You'd be better occupied thinking about your own future than worrying about mine. What you're going to do next week. The money you've got stashed in your underwear isn't going to last very long when you're out there on your own.'

Reminding her that she might have found a temporary sanctuary, but that was all it was.

Reminding himself.

Annie let out a long silent breath as he walked away, but it had more to do with the anger, the pain that had come off him like a blast of ice than fear that he'd seen through her disguise.

Although maybe, she thought, looking down at the glasses in her hand, maybe she should be worrying about that.

She'd assumed that he'd pushed the paper at her so that she could check out her 'double'. Think about the career opportunities it offered. But he hadn't actually said that.

Even with the evidence that she wasn't the 'people's virgin'—and could it be any more lowering than to have her lack of sexual experience pitied by a sixteen-year-old?—on the table in front of her.

She was in Bab el Sama. It said so right there for the whole world to see, yet still he'd handed her back her disguise as if he thought she needed it.

Too late for that, she thought, dropping the glasses into her bag and switching on her cellphone to thumb in a quick text to Lydia.

Tomorrow there would have to be pictures to prove she was there.

'Are you all right, dear?' The woman who'd served them came to clear the table and wipe it down and glanced after George meaningfully.

'I'm fine,' she said, switching off the phone. 'Honestly.'

'Christmas...' she said, sighing as Rudolph started up yet again. 'It's all stress. You wouldn't believe the things I hear. Did you know that there are more marriage break-ups over Christmas than at any other time of year?'

'Really? I'll bear that in mind. Should I ever get married.'

'Oh… You and he aren't…?'

'We only met yesterday, but thank you for caring,' Annie said, stowing her phone and standing up. 'Being ready to listen. That's the true spirit of the season.'

'The Christmas fairy, that's me,' she said with an embarrassed laugh before whisking away the tray.

And nothing wrong with that, Annie thought, before crossing to the window to see how far things had progressed.

One of the trees had already been hoisted onto the roof of the car, but as George and a good-looking boy bent to lift the second, larger tree, Xandra, who had climbed up to lash the first into place, stopped what she was doing and looked down, not at the boy, but at her father.

Full of longing, need, it was a look that she recognised, understood and she forgot her own concerns as her heart went out to the girl.

They'd both lost their parents, but in Xandra's case the situation wasn't irretrievable. Her mother might not be perfect but she'd be home in a few weeks. And George was here right now, bringing the scent of fresh spruce with him as he returned to the chalet to pay for the trees.

For once it didn't bring a lump to her throat, the ache of unbearable memories. This wasn't her Christmas, but Xandra's. A real celebration to share with the grandparents she adored. And with George, if he took his chance and seized the opportunity to change things.

'All done?' she asked.

He gave her a look that suggested she had to be joking. 'This is just the beginning. When we get back I'm going to have to find suitable containers and erect them safely so that they don't topple over if the cat decides to go climbing.'

'Back', not home, she noticed. He never called the house he'd grown up in 'home'.

'Then I'll have to sort out lights and check them to make sure they won't blow all the fuses.'

'Why don't you ask that boy to give you a hand?' she suggested. 'Earn yourself some Brownie points with your daughter.'

'I don't think so,' he said, handing a grubby hand-written docket to the woman behind the till along with some banknotes.

Protective. A good start, she thought.

'You can't keep her wrapped in cotton wool.' At least not without the kind of money that would make Dower House fees look like chicken feed. 'And, even if you could, she wouldn't thank you for it.'

'Nothing new there, then,' he said, slotting the

pound coins the woman gave him as change into a charity box on the counter.

They piled back into the car and this time Xandra gave her more room so she wasn't squashed up against George. Just close enough to be tinglingly aware of every movement. For his hand to brush her thigh each time he changed gear.

'We'll need to stop at the garden centre in Long-bourne to pick up some bags of compost,' Xandra said carelessly as he paused at the farm gate. 'If the trees are to have a chance of surviving.'

'I don't think—'

'Granddad always plants out the Christmas trees,' she said stubbornly.

'I remember,' he muttered under his breath so that only she heard. Then, raising his voice above the sound of the engine, 'He won't be fit enough to do it this year, Xandra.'

Her eyes widened a little as the reality of her grandfather's heart attack truly hit home, but then she shrugged. 'It's not a problem. I can do it.'

'Damn you!' George banged the steering wheel with the flat of his hand. 'You are just like him, do you know that? Stubborn, pig-headed, deaf to reason…'

Xandra's only response was to switch on the personal stereo in her jacket pocket and stick in her earplugs.

George didn't say a word and Annie kept her

own mouth firmly shut as they pulled into the garden centre car park.

It was one of those out of town places and it had a huge range of house plants that had been forced for the holiday, as well as every kind of seasonal decoration imaginable.

While George disappeared in search of compost, Annie used the time to pick out a dark pink cyclamen for Hetty and Xandra disappeared into the Christmas grotto.

When they met at the till ten minutes later she was half hidden behind an armful of decorations in just about every colour imaginable—none of that colour co-ordination nonsense for her—and wearing a three-foot-long Santa hat.

CHAPTER NINE

ANNIE, desperate to find some way to make George see beyond the defence mechanism that his daughter was using to save herself from the risk of hurt, was so deep in thought as she pushed open the kitchen door with her shoulder that the spicy scent of the Christmas cake baking took her unawares.

A punch to the heart.

Like the fresh, zingy scent of the trees, it evoked only painful memories and the armful of tinsel she was carrying slithered to the floor as she came to a dead stop.

'What's wrong?' George asked, following her in.

She tried to speak, couldn't. Instead, she shook her head and, giving herself time to recover, she bent to scoop up the glittering strands, only to find herself face to face with George as he joined her down at floor level.

'What is it?' he asked quietly as he took the pot plant from her.

'Nothing. It's nothing.' Dredging up a smile—a

lady never showed her feelings—she wound a thick gold strand of tinsel around his neck. 'Just blinded by all this glitter,' she said, clutching it to her as she made a move to stand.

He caught her by the wrist, keeping her where she was.

'G-George…' she begged, her voice hoarse with the effort of keeping up the smile.

'You will tell me,' he warned her, his own smile just as broad, just as false as her own as he took a purple strand of tinsel and slowly wrapped it, once, twice around her throat before, his hand still tightly around her wrist, he drew her to her feet.

'Oh, well, there's a picture,' Hetty said, laughing as she caught sight of them. 'Did you buy up their entire stock, Xan?'

'You can never have too much tinsel,' she said as she trailed in with the rest of it.

'Is that right?' She took her coat from the hook and said, 'I'll be off now, if you don't mind, Annie. The cake should be done by one-thirty. I've set the timer. Just stick a skewer in the centre and if it comes out clean you can take it out.' She put on her gloves, found her car keys and picked up a bag laden with treats for the invalid. 'I've made vegetable soup for lunch. Just help yourself.'

'Can I do something about dinner?' Annie asked.

George, giving her a look that suggested she was kidding herself, said, 'Why don't I get a takeaway?'

'Oh, great!' Xandra said, sorting through the tinsel and finding a heavy strand in shocking pink and throwing it around herself like a boa. 'Can we have Chinese? Please, please, please…'

'Annie?' he asked, turning to her.

'I couldn't think of anything I'd like more,' she said and got a quizzical look for her pains. She ignored it. 'I hope Mr Saxon will be feeling better today, Hetty.'

'Can I come with you?' Xandra asked. 'I could decorate his bed. Cheer him up.'

'I don't think they'll let you do that. Decorations would get in the way if…' Her voice faltered momentarily before she forced a smile. 'And what about this tree you've bought? You can't leave your father to put it up by himself.'

'Trees. We bought two, but they'll wait until the morning.'

'Will they? But if you come with me you'll be stuck in the hospital all day. And, besides, Granddad will want to know why you're home. I don't think it'll do his heart any good if he finds out you've been suspended from school, young lady.'

'He wouldn't care. He thinks Dower House is a total waste of money.'

'Your grandfather always did believe that education is for wimps,' George said. Then, clearly wishing he'd kept his mouth shut, he said, 'Go with your grandmother—'

'George—'

'I'll pick her up when I've finished the Bentley,' he said, glancing at his watch. 'Three o'clock? Be waiting outside. I'm not coming in to fetch you.'

'Congratulations, George,' Annie said when they'd gone. 'You came within a cat's whisker of behaving like a father for a moment, but you managed to rescue the situation before you could be mistaken for anyone who gives a damn.'

Furious with him for missing such a chance, she crossed to the stove, took the lid off the soup and banged it on the side.

'Pass me a bowl if you want some of this,' she said, sticking out a hand.

He put a bowl in it without a word and she filled the ladle with the thick soup, only to find her hand was shaking so much that she couldn't hold it. She dropped it back in the saucepan and George grabbed the bowl before she dropped that too.

'Damn you,' she said, hanging onto the rail that ran along the front of the oven. 'Would it have hurt you so much to spend a few minutes with your father? Have you any idea how lucky you are to have him? Have a mother who cares enough to make your favourite food?'

She turned to face him. He was still wearing the tinsel and he should have looked ridiculous. The truth was that he could have been wearing a pair of glass tree baubles dangling from his ears and Xandra's Santa hat and he'd still melt her bones.

That didn't lessen her anger.

'What did he do to you?' she asked. 'Why do you hate him so much?'

'It's what he didn't do that's the problem, but this isn't about me, is it?'

He reached out, touched her cheek, then held up his fingers so that she could see that they were wet.

'Why are you crying, Annie?'

'For the waste. The stupid waste…' Then, dragging in a deep, shuddering breath, she shook her head and rubbed her palms over her face to dry tears she hadn't been conscious of shedding. 'I'm sorry. You're right. I've no right to shout at you. I know nothing about what happened between you and your father. It's just this time of year. It's just…'

She stalled, unable to even say the word.

'It's just Christmas,' he said. 'I saw the way you reacted when you walked into the kitchen. As if you'd been struck. Spice, nuts, fruit, brandy. It's the quintessential smell of the season. And scent evokes memory as nothing else can.'

She opened her mouth, closed it. Swallowed.

'You think you're alone in hating it?'

She shook her head. Took a long, shuddering breath. Then, realising what he'd said, she looked up. 'Xandra said you hate Christmas. Said she knew why.'

'I came home for Christmas at the end of my

first term at university to be met with the news that Penny was pregnant. My father was delighted, in case you're wondering. He thought I'd have to give up all thought of university and join him in the business. He was going to build us a house in the paddock, give me a partnership—'

'And you turned him down.'

'Penny thought, once we were actually married—and believe me, there's nothing like a shotgun wedding to add a little cheer for Christmas—that she could persuade me to change my mind.' He managed a wry smile. 'I've never eaten Christmas cake since.'

She stared at him, then realised that he was joking. Making light of a desperate memory. She wondered just how much pressure—emotional and financial—he'd endured.

'You didn't have to marry her. People don't these days.'

'It was my responsibility. My baby.'

She reached out to him. Touched his big, capable hand. Afraid for him.

If Xandra had inherited just one tenth of his stubborn determination, she feared they were heading for the kind of confrontation that could shatter any hope of reconciliation.

'What happened to you, Annie?' he asked. 'What are you really running away from?'

'Apart from Christmas?'

'There's no escape from that,' he said, 'unless, like Lady Rose Napier, you can borrow a palace from a friend.'

How ironic was that? She'd sent Lydia to a Christmas free zone, while she'd found herself in tinsel land.

'How is it on a Californian beach?' she asked in an attempt to head off the big question.

'Sunny, but it's not the weather, or the decorations or the carols. The trouble with Christmas is that, no matter how high the presents are piled, it shines a light into the empty spaces. Highlights what's missing from your life.' He curved his palm around her cheek. 'What's missing from yours, Annie?'

His touch was warm, his gentle voice coaxing and somehow the words were out before she could stop them.

'My parents. They were killed a week before the holiday. They were away and I was fizzing with excitement, waiting for them to come home so that we could decorate the tree, but they never came.'

There was an infinitesimal pause as he absorbed this information. 'Was it a road accident?'

They had been on a road. Four innocent people who, in the true spirit of Christmas, had been taking aid to a group of desperate people. Food, medicine, clothes, toys even. She'd sent her favourite doll for them to give to some poor homeless, starving child.

She wanted to tell him all that, but she couldn't

because then he'd know who she was and she'd have to leave. And she didn't want to leave.

'They were passengers,' she said. 'Two other people with them died, too.' She never forgot them or their families, who went through this same annual nightmare as she did. 'They were buried on the day before Christmas Eve and then everything went on as if nothing had changed. The tree lights were turned on, there were candles in the church on Christmas morning, presents after tea. It was what they would have expected, I was told. Anything else would be letting them down.'

And then there had been the Boxing Day shoot.

She looked up at George. 'Every year it's as if I'm six years old,' she said, trying to make him understand. 'The tree, church, unwrapping presents. Going through the motions, smiling because it's expected and every year that makes me a little bit more—' she clenched her fists, trying to catch the word, but it spilled over, unstoppable '—angry.'

She didn't know where that had come from, but it was as if at that moment a dam had burst and all the pent-up emotion of the last twenty years burst out.

'I hate it,' she said, banging on his chest with her bunched fists. 'Hate the carols...' Bang... 'Hate the lights...' Bang... 'The falseness...' He caught her wrists.

'Is that what you're really running away from, Annie?' he asked, holding her off.

'Yes.' She pulled back, shaking her head as she crumpled against the stove and slid to the floor. 'No…'

George didn't try to coax her up, but kept hold of her hands, going down with her, encouraging her to lean against him so that her cheek was against the hard fabric of his overalls.

'No,' he agreed.

He smelled of engine oil, spruce, some warmer scent that was George himself that mingled to make something new, something that held no bad memories for her, and she let her head fall against his chest.

'You can run away from Christmas, Annie, but you can't escape what it is you hate about it. The bad memories.'

'I thought if I could just get away for a while, see things from a different perspective,' she said after a while, 'I might find a way to deal with it. But you're right. It's nothing to do with the season. It simply shines a light on everything that's wrong in our lives.'

George held her, her hair against his cheek, thinking about an unhappy little girl who had spent year after year being brave for the adults who clearly hadn't a clue how to cope with her grief. And he wondered whether his daughter's desperate need to decorate every surface for the holiday exposed the emptiness at the heart of her life too.

'We are what circumstances make us,' he said, leaning back. 'My father used to make me work in the garage. Every day, after school, he set me a task that I had to finish before I was allowed to go and get on with my homework.'

He knew she'd turned to look up at him, but he kept staring ahead, remembering how it had been.

Remembering the weeks, months, years when anger had kept him going.

'I learned fast.' He'd had to if he was to defeat his father. 'He set me ever more complex, time-consuming tasks, reasoning that if I failed at school I would have no choice but to stay here, so that he could be George Saxon and not just the "and Son".'

By the time he'd been old enough to work that out, pity him, the battle lines were drawn and there was no going back.

'If I inherited one thing from my old man it was obstinacy. I got up early, worked late. Learned to manage on the minimum of sleep. And when I left for university I was the best mechanic in the garage, including my father. He never forgave me for that.'

Finally he looked down at her, not quite believing that he was sharing his most painful memories with a woman he'd picked up on the side of the road the evening before.

Could scarcely believe that sitting here, on the floor of his mother's kitchen with his arm around her, was the nearest he'd come to peace for as long as he could remember.

'And you still found time for girls?'

'That last summer, before I went up to university, I found time for a lot of things that I'd missed out on.' Life at home might have been unbearable, but there had been compensations. 'The minute I turned eighteen, I got a job at a garage that paid me what I was actually worth.'

'Your poor mother. It must have been as restful as living with two big cats walking stiff-legged around one another, hackles raised.'

He smiled. 'Don't tell me, you were the fly on the wall?'

'I've spent a lot of my life watching people. I can read body language as well as I read English.'

He must have shown a flicker of dismay because she laughed. 'Most body language. There are gaps in my knowledge.'

'What kind of gaps?'

She shook her head. 'Tell me what you did. After you'd turned your back on the "and Son". What paid for the California beach house? The fees for Dower House?'

'I knew two things—software engineering and cars—so I put them together and developed a software application for the motor industry. My father disapproves of computers on principle. Driving, for him, is a question of man and machine—nothing in between. So he never forgave me for that, either.'

'Maybe you have to forgive yourself first,' she said.

Forgive himself?

For a moment his brain floundered with the concept, but only for a moment. Annie was looking up at him, smiling a little as if she knew something he didn't. The tears she'd shed had added a sparkle to her eyes and as her lips parted to reveal a glimpse of perfect teeth he forgot what she'd said, knew only that he wanted to kiss her, was trembling with the need to kiss her in a way he hadn't since he was eighteen years old and Penny Lomax had made a man of him.

'Who are you?' he demanded, but as she opened her mouth to answer him he covered it with his hand.

'No. Don't tell me. I don't want to know.'

He didn't want her to tell him anything that would stop him from kissing her, from doing what he'd wanted to do ever since she'd stumbled into him and her scent had taken up residence in his head.

Fluent in body language, she knew exactly what he was thinking and didn't wait, but reached up and pulled him down to her, coming up to meet him with a raw to-hell-and-back kiss that said only one thing.

I want you. I need you.

Her other hand, clutching at his shoulder, her nails digging through the heavy material of his overalls, proclaimed the urgency of that need.

The heat of it shuddered through him, igniting a flame that would have taken an ice-cold shower to cool. Sitting by a solid-fuel stove, they didn't stand a chance, even if he'd wanted one, he thought, tugging her shirt free of her jeans and reaching inside it to unhook the fastening of her bra. He half expected a bundle of twenty-pound notes to cascade out of it but, as he slid his hand inside it, it was filled with nothing more than a small, firm breast.

She moaned into his mouth, tearing at the studs on his overalls, her touch electric as she pushed up the T-shirt he was wearing beneath it before drawing back a little to look up at him, her eyes shining like hot sapphires, silently asking permission to touch him.

He shrugged his arms out of his overalls, pulled off the T-shirt he was wearing beneath it and fell back against the thick rag rug that had lain in that spot for as long as he could remember.

'Help yourself,' he said, grinning as he offered himself up to her.

Her fingers stopped a tantalising hair's breadth from his skin.

'What can I do?'

Do?

'Anything…' he began, then caught his breath as her fingertips made contact with his chest. 'Anything that feels good,' he managed, through a throat apparently stuffed with cobwebs. 'Good for you,' he added and he nearly lost it as they trailed down his chest, her long nails grazing the hollow of his stomach.

For a moment, as she straightened, he thought she'd changed her mind, but she caught the hem of her sweater and pulled it, shirt and bra over her head and discarded them impatiently. Her long body was taut, strong, her breasts were high, firm, beautiful and her eyes widened in shock and a shiver ran through her body as he touched a nipple.

'You like that?' he asked.

She made an unintelligible sound that was pure delight and, seizing her around the waist, he lifted her so that she straddled his body, wanting her to know that he liked it too. To feel his heat, know what she was doing to him. Had been doing to him since the moment she'd pitched into his arms.

For a moment she didn't move, then, with the tiniest of sighs, she bent to lay her lips against his stomach and this time the moan came from him.

'You like that?' she asked mischievously, looking up with the smile of a child who'd just been given the freedom of a sweet shop. Then he was the one catching his breath as she leaned forward to touch her lips to his, her breasts brushing his chest. He wanted to crush her to him, overwhelm her, cut short the teasing foreplay, but some things were too good to rush and this was going to be very good indeed.

As she took her lips on a slow trail of moist kisses over his chin, down his throat, he held her in the very lightest of touches, his hands doing no more than rest against her ribcage, giving her control, all the time, all the freedom she wanted to explore his body, knowing that his time would come.

Little feathers of silky hair brushed against his skin, a subtle counterpoint to her tongue probing the hollows beneath his shoulders, to the satiny feel of her skin as his hands slid lower over her back, exploring the curve of her waist, learning the shape of her body.

Annie was drowning in pure sensation. The gentle touch of George's hands as he caressed her back, her waist, slipping beneath the loose waist of her jeans to cup her bottom in his hands, holding her close so that she could feel the power of his need as she kissed and licked and nibbled at his chest, the hollow of his stomach. Came against the barrier of clothes.

Her lips were hot, swollen against his skin and every cell in her body was thrumming with power. For the first time in her life she felt totally alive, warm, vital. This ache in her womb, this need was the essence of life, of being a woman and she wanted him. Wanted all of him.

'Touch me,' she whispered as she pulled at the next stud.

Begging or commanding?

It didn't matter. He'd told her she could do anything that felt good. And this felt...

He released the button at the waist of her jeans, pushed jeans, underwear over her hips.

There were no words to describe what this felt like. All she could manage was his name.

'George…'

And then her body shattered.

George caught her, held her as she collapsed against him, kissing her shoulder, nuzzling his chin against her hair as she recovered, trying not to think about the look in her eyes, an appeal for something unknown, in that moment before she'd dissolved into his arms.

Because he knew where he'd see it before.

He murmured her name and when she looked up, her eyes filled with tears, he knew it was true. She was the 'people's virgin'.

'Will I get sent to the Tower for that?' he asked.

'Not by me,' she assured him, laughing shakily.

Damn it, she was crying with gratitude.

She sniffed. Brushed the tears from her cheeks with the palm of her hand, lifted damp lashes and finally realised that he wasn't laughing with her.

'What?' she asked. 'What did I do?'

He didn't answer and he saw the exact moment when she realised that she answered not to the lie she'd told him when she'd sworn that Annie was her real name, but to Lady Rose.

'Rose*anne*,' she said. 'My name is Rose*anne*. I was named for my grandmother but my mother thought I was entitled to a name of my own so she called me Annie.'

Did she think that was all that mattered? That she hadn't actually lied about that.

Then, when he didn't answer, 'Does it matter?'

He picked up the clothes she'd discarded and thrust them at her.

'George?'

For a long moment she didn't take them but continued to look at him, those dangerous eyes pleading with him.

All his senses were vibrating with the feel of her, her touch, the musky scent of her most intimate being. They were urging him to say that it didn't matter a damn before reaching out to take what she was offering him. Pretend that nothing mattered but this moment.

The shattering sound of the timer announcing that the cake was done saved them both.

'Clearly it does,' she said, snatching her clothes from his hand, standing up, turning her back on him as she pulled them on.

'You used me,' he said to her back. 'You're on a quest to lose your virginity before you settle for the guy with the castle.'

'If that's what you think then there's nothing more to say. Pass me the oven gloves,' she said, sticking out a hand as she opened the oven door.

He got up, passed her the thickly padded gloves, then pulled the overalls back on, fastening the studs with shaking fingers while, still with her back to him, she tested the cake.

'Is it done?'

'As if you care,' she replied, still not looking at him but turning the cake out over the rack his mother had left out. When the cake didn't fall out she gave it a shake, catching her breath as the hot tin touched the pale skin of her inner arm.

'You have to leave it to cool for a few minutes,' he said, taking her hand, turning it to look at the red mark.

'I get cookery lessons too?'

'Simple physics,' he said, not bothering to ask her if it hurt, just grabbing her hand and taking her to the sink, where he turned on the cold tap, holding the burn beneath the running water.

It was icy-cold and he knew that would hurt as much as the burn but she clamped her jaws together. Schooled from the age of six not to show pain, she'd saved her tears for him.

It had taken the new, shocking pleasure of a man's intimate touch to break down that reserve, reduce her to weeping for herself.

'Who is she?' he asked, not wanting to think about how that made him feel. Feeling would destroy him. 'The girl in the photograph.'

'Lydia,' she said.

'The friend who lent you her car? But she—'

'Looks just like me? Type "Lady Rose" and "lookalike" into your search engine and you can book her next time you want "Lady Rose Napier" to grace your party.'

'Why would I want a copy…?'

He managed to stop himself but she finished for him. 'Why would you want a copy when you rejected the real thing?'

She was shaking, he realised. Or maybe it was him.

'She's a professional lookalike?'

'Since she was fifteen years old. Her mother made her a copy of the outfit I was wearing on my sixteenth birthday and someone took a picture and sent it to the local newspaper. It's not a full-time job for her, of course, but the manager of the supermarket where she works is very good about juggling her shifts.'

'You paid a girl who works in a supermarket to take your place?'

'No. She wouldn't take any money. We met by chance one day and there was a connection.'

'I'll bet there was. Do you really trust her not to sell her story to the tabloids the minute she gets home?'

She looked up at him. 'Do you know something, George? I don't really care. I wanted to escape and she was willing to take my place so that I could disappear without raising a hue and cry. Once I go back I don't care who knows.'

'But how on earth will she carry it off? It's one thing turning up at a party where everyone knows you're not the real thing, but something like this…' Words failed him.

'There's no one at Bab el Sama who knows me. I insisted on going there on my own.'

'But if you wanted a break, surely—'

'I wanted a break from being me, George. From my grandfather's unspoken expectations. I wanted to be ordinary. Just be…myself.'

'How is that?' he asked, gently dabbing her arm dry.

'I can't feel a thing.'

He nodded. 'I've got a car to fix,' he said, tossing the towel aside, wishing he could say the same.

He walked from the room while he still could.

CHAPTER TEN

ANNIE, weak to her bones, leaned against the sink. What had she done, said, to give herself away?

A tear trickled onto her cheek and as she palmed it away she knew. He'd responded to her not as a national institution but as a woman and she'd wept with the joy of it. Ironic, really, when she'd spent her entire life keeping her emotions under wraps.

Tears were private things.

Before the cameras you kept your dignity, looked the world in the eye.

But with a lover you could be yourself. Utterly, completely…

A long shivering sigh escaped her but the years of training stood her in good stead. She took a deep breath, straightened, told herself that George had every right to be angry.

What man, on discovering that what he'd imagined was a quick tumble in the metaphorical hay had the potential to make him front-page news, wouldn't be absolutely livid?

She might be inexperienced, but she wasn't naïve.

Sex exposed two people in a way that nothing else could. It wasn't the nakedness, but the stripping away of pretence that took it beyond the purely physical. Without total honesty it was a sham, a lie.

She knew how she'd feel if he'd lied to her about his identity. But he'd laid it all out while she hadn't even been honest about the way her parents had died.

She had abused his trust in the most fundamental way and now she would have to leave. First, though, she carefully turned out the cake and left it to cool. Washed the cake tin. Put away the soup bowls.

Straightened the rag rug.

When all trace of her presence had been erased, she went upstairs and threw everything into her bag. Then, because she couldn't leave without saying goodbye to Xandra, she walked along the hall, opening doors, searching for her room, and found herself standing in the doorway of the room in which George Saxon had grown up.

The cashmere sweater he'd been wearing the day before was draped over the wooden chair. She touched it, then picked it up, hugging it to her as she looked around at what had been his boyhood room.

It was sparse by modern standards, with none of the high-tech appliances that were the essential requirements of the average teen's life. Just a narrow bed with an old-fashioned quilt, a small scarred table he'd used as a desk and a bookcase. She knelt to run her fingers over the spines of the books he'd held, read. Physics, maths, computer languages.

The car maintenance manuals seemed out of place, but keeping ahead of his father must have required more than manual dexterity, although personally she'd have given him a starred A for that.

She stood up, holding the sweater to her face for a moment, yearning to pull it over her head and walk away with it. Instead, she refolded it and laid it back on the chair before leaving the room, closing the door behind her.

Xandra's room was next door. Large, comfortable, a total contrast to her father's childhood room, it was obvious that she spent a lot of time with her grandparents.

She had a small colour television, an expensive laptop, although the girlish embroidered bed cover was somewhat at odds with the posters of racing drivers rather than pop stars that decorated the walls.

There was paper and a pen on the writing desk and a note to Mrs Warburton ready for the post.

She picked up the pen, then put it down again. What could she say? She couldn't tell her the truth and she couldn't bear to write a lie. Better to leave George to make whatever excuses he thought best.

Downstairs, she'd looked up the number of a taxi firm and made the call. She'd catch a bus or a train; it didn't matter where to, so long as it was leaving Maybridge.

'It's a busy time of the day,' the dispatcher warned her. 'It'll be half an hour before we can pick you up.'

'That will be fine,' she said. It wasn't, but if it was a busy time she'd get the same response from anyone else. As she replaced the receiver, the cat found her legs and she bent to pick it up, ruffling it behind the ear as she carried it into the study to wait in the chair where George had fallen asleep the night before. Self-indulgently resting her head in the place where his had been.

The cat settled on her lap, purring contentedly and she closed her eyes for a moment, letting herself rerun images of George's body, his face as he'd looked at her, the taste of his skin, his lips, the way he'd touched her. Fixing it like a film in her memory so that she would be able to take it out and run it like a video when she needed to remind herself what it was like to just let go.

'Annie!'

She woke with a start as the cat dug its claws into her legs before fleeing.

It took her a moment for her head to clear, to focus on George standing in the doorway. 'Sorry, I must have fallen asleep. Is my taxi here?'

'Were you going to leave without a word?' he demanded.

'What word did you expect? I can't stay here, George. Not now you know who I am.'

He didn't bother to deny it. 'Where are you going?'

'That's none of your business.'

'You think?' He moved so swiftly that she didn't have time to do more than think about moving before his hands were on either side of her, pinning her in the chair. 'Do you really believe I'm going to let the nation's sweetheart wander off into the wild blue yonder by herself with a fistful of money stuffed down her bra?'

He was close enough that she could see the vein throbbing at his temple, the tiny sparks of hot anger that were firing the lead grey of his eyes, turning it molten.

'I don't think you have a choice.'

'Think again, Your Ladyship. I've got a whole heap of options open to me, while you've got just two. One, you stay here where I know you're safe. Two, I take you home to your grandfather, His Grace the Duke of Oldfield. Take your pick.'

'You've been checking up on me?'

'You're not the only one with a fancy Internet cellphone.'

Obviously he had. Searched for her on the Net instead of asking. Maybe he thought that was the only way to get straight answers. Her fault.

'And if I don't fancy either of those options?' she asked, refusing to be browbeaten into capitulation. 'You said you had a whole heap?'

'I could ring around the tabloids and tell them what you've been doing for the last twenty-four hours.'

'You wouldn't do that.' He'd hesitated for a fraction of a second before he'd spoken and instinctively she lifted her hand to his face. His cold cheek warmed to her touch. His eyes darkened. 'You wouldn't betray me, George.'

'Try me,' he said, abruptly straightening, taking a step back, putting himself out of reach. Pulling the shutters down, just as he had with Xandra. 'Anything could happen to you out there. Use a little of your famous empathy to consider how I'd feel if anything did.'

'I'm not your responsibility.'

'You can't absolve me of that. I know who you are. That changes everything.'

'I'm sorry,' she said.

'Prove it.'

'By going home or staying here until the seventeenth?'

'The seventeenth?' He looked hunted, as if the prospect of a whole week of her company appalled him, but he said, 'If that's your time frame, then yes. Take your pick.'

'It's a long time to put up with a stranger.' And a

long time to spend with a man who despised you. 'If you let me go I'll be careful,' she promised.

'Would that be reversing-into-a-farm-gate-in-the-dark careful?'

'I'll use public transport.'

'That's supposed to reassure me? You stay here or you go home,' he said. 'It's not open for discussion.'

'What would you say to your mother if I stayed?'

'She's got more important things to worry about. This is just between us,' he warned. 'As far as Xandra and my mother are concerned, you're Annie Rowland. Is that understood?'

'You guessed who I was,' she pointed out.

'I don't think they're ever going to see you quite the way I did.'

'No?' She felt a tremor deep within her at the memory of just how he'd seen her. Remembered how powerful she'd felt as he'd looked at her, touched her. As she'd touched him. She wanted that again. Wanted him… 'If I stay, George,' she asked softly, 'will you finish what you started?'

He opened his mouth, then shut it again sharply. Shook his head.

No. Faced with her image, he was just like everyone else. Being the nation's virgin was, apparently, the world's biggest turn-off.

'It's just sex, George,' she said, hoping that she could provoke him, disgust him sufficiently so that he would let her go.

'If it's just sex, Annie, I'm sure Rupert Devenish would be happy to do you the favour. Put it on the top of your Christmas wish list. Or does he have to wait until he puts a ring on your finger? Were you simply looking for something a little more earthy than His Lordship before you settle for the coronet?'

If he'd actually hit her the shock couldn't have been more brutal. It wasn't the suggestion that she was on the loose looking for a bit of rough. It was the fact that he thought she'd marry for position, the castle, the estates, that drove through her heart like a dagger. And maybe the fear that, in desperation, six months, a year from now she might settle for the chance to be a mother.

Picking up the phone, admitting what she'd done and waiting for a car to take her home would, she knew without doubt, be the first step.

It took her a moment to gather herself, find her voice. 'I'd better go and pay the taxi.'

'It's done.'

'What?' Then, realising what he meant, 'You sent it away without waiting for my answer?'

'He's busy. You owe me twenty pounds, by the way.'

'A little more than that, surely? There's the call-out charge, towing me back to the garage, the time you spent on the car.' She looked up enquiringly when he didn't answer. 'Or shall I ask Xandra to prepare the invoice for that?'

'Forget it,' he said. 'The garage is closed. And forget the taxi fare too.'

'What about board and lodging? Or do you expect me to work for my keep?'

'You are my daughter's guest,' he said, glancing at his watch. 'And right now we have to go and pick her up.'

'We?'

'You don't imagine I'm going to leave you here on your own?'

She thought about arguing with him for all of a second before she said, 'I'll get my coat.'

Two minutes later she was wrapped in the soft leather of the sports car that had been parked on the garage forecourt and heading towards Maybridge General.

They exchanged barely two words as the car ate up the miles but, when he pulled into the pick-up bay a couple of minutes before three, Annie said, 'There's a parking space over there.'

'It's nearly three. Xandra will be here any minute.'

She didn't say a word.

'Are you suggesting that she won't?'

'I'm suggesting that she'll make you go and get her, so you might as well make a virtue out of a necessity.'

'I could send you.'

'You could. But then you'd have to come and get

me too. Always supposing I don't take the opportunity to leave by another entrance.'

'Without your bag?'

'I could replace everything in it in ten minutes.'

'A thousand pounds won't go far if you're travelling by public transport. Staying at hotels.'

Again she said nothing.

'There's more? How much?'

'You'll have to search me to discover that,' she said, glancing at him. 'I won't resist.'

His hands tightened on the steering wheel, the knuckles turning white.

'Go and visit your father. It would make your mother happy, make Xandra happy. And me. It would make me very happy.'

'And why would I give a damn whether you're happy or not?'

He was so stubborn. He knew it was the right thing to do, wanted to build bridges with his daughter, but pride kept him from taking that first step. She'd just have to give him a little push.

'Because, if you don't, George, I'll be the one calling the tabloids to tell them that Lady Rose isn't in Bab el Sama but holed up at Saxon's Garage. With her lover.'

'Lover!'

'Why spoil a good story by telling the truth?' she said. 'They certainly won't.'

'You wouldn't do that.'

Exactly what she'd said when he'd threatened her.

'Within an hour of our return from the hospital there'll be television crews, photographers and half the press pack on your doorstep.'

'They wouldn't believe you. They've seen you get on a plane.'

'So what? You were bluffing?'

'Of course I was bluffing!'

He cared, she thought. Cared enough.

So did she.

'Take your pick, George. Visit your father or let me go.'

George dragged both hands through his hair. 'I can't. Please, Annie, you must see that. If anything happened to you—'

'You'd never forgive yourself? Oh, dear. That is unfortunate because, you see, I'm not bluffing. And I know those journalists well enough to convince them I'm not some fantasist sending them on a wild-goose chase.' She held her breath. Would he believe her? After what seemed like the longest moment in history, he glared at her, then pulled over into the empty space she'd pointed out. Cut the engine.

'This isn't going to work,' he said, releasing his seat belt, climbing out. 'Whatever it is you think you're doing.' She jumped as he vented his frustration on the car door, but made no move to get out, forcing him to walk around to the passenger door and open it for her.

George watched as she swung her long legs over the sill, stood up and, without a word, walked towards the entrance of the hospital.

'You know that's a dead giveaway too,' he said when he caught up with her. 'Modern independent women can usually manage a car door.'

'If you insist on acting as my bodyguard, George, I'll insist on treating you like one.'

'Remind me why they call you the nation's sweetheart?' he said.

'Sweetheart, angel, virgin.' She stopped without warning and looked at him, a tiny frown wrinkling her smooth forehead. '*Am* I still the people's virgin?' she asked, her clear voice carrying down the corridor. 'Technically?'

'Annie!' He grabbed her elbow in an attempt to hurry her past a couple of nurses who'd turned to stare. 'What the hell do you think you're doing?'

'Behaving badly?' she offered, staying stubbornly put. 'It's a new experience for me and I'm rather enjoying it. But you didn't answer my question. Am I—'

'Don't say another word,' he snapped. He didn't want to talk about it. Or think about it. Fat chance. He hadn't been able to think about anything else all afternoon and while his head was saying no, absolutely no, a thousand times no, his body was refusing to listen. 'It's this way.'

But it wasn't. His father had improved sufficiently to be moved out of the cardiac suite and into a small ward. Xandra was sitting cross-legged on the bed, Santa hat perched on her head, while his father occupied an armchair beside it. He was laughing at something she'd said and it was obvious that they were on the same wavelength, despite the generation gap. That they liked one another. Were friends. Everything that he and his father were not. Everything that he and his daughter were not.

They both froze as they saw him.

'I was just coming,' Xandra said, immediately defensive.

'No problem,' he lied. 'We were a bit early.'

'Is this Annie?' his father asked, looking beyond him. 'Xandra's been telling me all about you.'

'Oh, dear…' she stepped forward, hand extended— a scene reminiscent of every news clip he'd ever seen of a royal hospital visit '…I don't like the sound of that!' Then, 'How d'you do, Mr Saxon?'

'I do very well, thank you,' he said. 'Certainly well enough to get out of here.'

'I'm glad to hear it.'

George wondered how many times she'd done that. Visited a total stranger in hospital, completely at ease, sure of her welcome.

'Xandra is a tonic,' he said. Then, finally turning to grudgingly acknowledge him, 'You've managed to drag yourself into the garage, I see.'

'Mike is picking up the Bentley in an hour.'

The nod his father managed was as close as he'd ever come to a thank you and he thought that was it, but he said, 'We've been looking after his cars ever since he started the business. I'm glad we didn't let him down.' And then he looked up. 'Thanks, son.'

The words were barely audible but he'd said them and it was George's turn to be lost for words.

It was Annie who broke the silence. 'Where's Hetty?'

'She went to the shop to get Granddad an evening paper,' Xandra said, watching them both.

'You could die of boredom in here,' his father said, with considerably more force in his voice than the day before. 'I don't care what that doctor says, I'm going home tomorrow.'

'Dad...' he protested.

'Your mother will take care of me,' he said stubbornly, the brief moment of rapport already history.

Annie's hand grabbed his before he let slip his first response, which was to tell him not to be so selfish.

'We'll all take care of you,' Xandra said quickly, looking at him, her eyes pleading with him to say that it would be all right. As if what he said actually mattered.

They were all taking tiny steps here and for a moment he clung to Annie's hand as if to a lifeline.

She squeezed his fingers, encouraging him to take the risk, throw his heart into the ring.

'If that's what you want,' he said, 'I'm sure we'll manage. Especially since Annie is staying on for a while to help out.'

'Really?' Xandra grinned. 'Great. You can help me put up the decorations.'

'Thank you,' Annie said, but she was looking at him. 'I'd like that.' Then, turning to his father, 'But you really must listen to the doctor, Mr Saxon. If you come home too soon, you'll be back in here for Christmas.'

His father regarded her thoughtfully. Then, taking note of the way their hands were interlinked and apparently putting one and one together and making a pair, he smiled with satisfaction. 'Maybe you're right, Annie. I don't suppose another day or two will kill me.'

Setting himself up for yet another disappointment that he'd get the blame for, George thought, and removing his hand from hers, he said, 'We'd better go, Xandra. Mike is coming for the car at four.'

She bounced off the bed, gave her granddad a hug. Then, transferring the Santa hat from her own head to his, she said, 'Behave yourself. And don't let Gran stay so late tonight. She was too tired to eat last night.'

'Really?' He shook his head. 'Silly woman. I'll make sure she leaves early.'

'Thanks for thinking about your gran,' he said as they headed for the car.

'She can't bear to leave him there on his own.' She turned to Annie. 'They absolutely dote on one another, you know. It's really sweet.' Then, taking advantage of his approval, she said, 'Can you drop me off in town? I'll catch the bus home.'

'I thought we'd decided that you're grounded.'

'Oh, absolutely,' she said. 'But this isn't for me. We've only got indoor lights. I'll have to get some new ones for the outside tree.' Then, 'Annie could come with me if you like. Just to make sure I don't have any fun.'

'Actually, I could do with a run at the shops,' Annie said before he could voice his objection to the idea of Lady Roseanne Napier, her underwear stuffed with cash and about as street-smart as a newborn lamb, let loose in the Christmas crowds with only a teenager for protection. 'I came away with the bare minimum.'

Oh, no...

The look in her eye told him she knew exactly what he was thinking.

'I'll do my absolute best to make sure that neither of us have any fun,' she assured him. 'Although I can't positively guarantee it.'

Xandra's face lit up. Annie did that to people, he thought. Lit them up. His mother, his father, his daughter. They all responded to that effortless charm, the natural warmth she exuded, but he'd done a lot more than just light up.

He'd lit up, overloaded, blown every fuse in his brain as he'd surrendered, had let down a barrier he'd been building against the world ever since the day when, years younger than Xandra, he'd understood that he was on his own.

Only now, when he knew that any kind of relationship between them was impossible, did he understand just how exposed he'd left himself.

Keeping his distance emotionally from this woman who was so far out of his orbit that he might as well be on Mars was now an absolute necessity. As was keeping her safe. But forbidding her to leave the house wasn't an option either.

'It's Friday so the shops will be open late, won't they?' he asked.

'I suppose.'

'In that case, if you're prepared to wait until after Mike's collected the Bentley, I'll take you both into town. We could pick up the takeaway on the way home.'

It sounded reasonable but he wasn't looking at Annie, knowing that she'd have raised that eyebrow a fraction, telling him that she was winning this stand-off hands down, instead concentrating on his daughter, willing her to say yes.

'You want to come shopping with us?' She sounded doubtful.

'Same deal as always,' he replied. 'I drive, you do the hard work.'

'That means you're going to have to carry your own bags to the car,' Annie said. 'Obviously, as a lady of rather more advanced years, I will expect him to carry mine.' She laid the lightest emphasis on the word 'lady'. She tilted an eyebrow at him. Taunting him. No, teasing him. 'Do you have a problem with that, George?'

'I can live with it,' he said, refusing to meet her gaze, afraid he might just break down and laugh. He was too angry with her to laugh. Too angry with himself for wanting to wrap his arms around her, hold her, kiss her, beg her never to leave because most of all he wanted her.

'What a hero,' she said gently. 'And the three of us could put up those trees while we're waiting.'

And right there and then, knowing that Christmas brought her a world of pain, he thought his heart might break that she would do that for his daughter. For him.

CHAPTER ELEVEN

THREE hours later, the car parked, her arm tucked firmly in George's—it was clear he wasn't going to let her stray from his side—Annie stood in the centre of Maybridge. There were lights everywhere and a brass band was playing Christmas carols as crowds of shoppers searched out presents for their loved ones.

Somewhere, in her subconscious, she knew this was how Christmas was meant to be, but now she was touching it, feeling it as she was jostled by shoppers laden with bags, excited children who'd spotted 'Santa' in a mock-up sleigh, collecting for a local charity. Noisy, joyful, it was a world away from Christmas as she knew it.

'What do you need?' George asked.

This. This normality. This man, she thought, as she looked up at him and for a moment the carols, the lights faded.

'Annie?'

This moment, she thought, refusing to think about next week.

'Just a few basic essentials. Underwear, another pair of jeans—these are a bit big,' she said, tugging at the waist. 'Nothing fancy.'

'I know just the place,' Xandra said. She paused at the entrance to a large store, glanced at her father. 'You might want to give this a miss.'

'If you think you can scare me away with threats of female undergarments, think again.'

'You are so embarrassing.'

'I understood it was a parent's duty to embarrass their offspring,' he replied, unmoved.

'Oh, please! I'll wait here,' she said, taking out her cellphone, her thumb already busy texting before she reached the nearest bench.

'I won't be long,' Annie said, then, realising that he wasn't going to let her out of his sight, proceeded to test his assertion. Faced with the choice between six-packs of pants in plain white, mixed colours or patterned, she asked him to choose.

He took all three packs and dropped them in the basket, lips firmly sealed.

She tried on jeans while he stood guard at the changing room door, modelling them for him. By the time they reached the socks he'd had enough and, after looking down at her feet, he gathered up a pair of each before she could tease him further.

'Spoilsport,' she said.

'You'd better believe it,' he said.

She added a sweater and three tops to the basket and then queued up to pay.

'That was fun,' she said, handing the bags to George and waving to Xandra before obediently slipping her hand through the elbow he'd stuck out. 'What now?'

'Food?' he suggested, heading for a van from which the tantalising smell of frying onions was wafting. 'Who fancies a hot dog?'

'Not for me,' Xandra said, backing away. 'I need some shampoo. Can I get you anything, Annie?'

'Please.' By the time she'd given Xandra some money, George had a halfeaten hot dog in one hand. 'Are they good?'

'You've never had one?' He shook his head. 'Stupid question.'

He ordered two. 'I missed lunch,' he said, catching her look as he sucked mustard from his thumb.

'Me too,' she said, holding his gaze as she took one of them from him.

He looked away first, which wasn't as pleasing as it should have been and, taking the only comfort on offer, she bit deep into the bun, reminding herself that she was in search of new experiences.

Who knew when she'd share another hot dog moment with a seriously sexy man?

It must have been the fumes of the mustard hitting the back of her throat that brought tears to her eyes, making her choke.

'Better?' George asked, helpfully thumping her back. Leaving his hand there.

'Not much,' she said, dropping the remains of the hot dog in the bin. 'It's been quite a day for new experiences.'

He removed his hand as if burned. 'What's keeping Xandra?'

She sighed. 'She said she'd meet us by the Christmas tree in the square.'

All the trees that surrounded the square had white lights threaded through their bare branches, creating a fairyland arena for the seasonal ice rink that had been created in the central plaza and throwing the huge Christmas tree, ablaze with colour, into vivid contrast.

But it wasn't the figures on the ice or the lights that brought George to an abrupt halt. It was the sight of his daughter, sitting on a bench, much too close to the boy from the Christmas tree farm.

'The damned lights were just an excuse to come into town and meet him,' he declared but, as he surged forward, Annie stepped in front of him, a hand on his chest.

'They could have met by chance.'

He looked at her. 'Do you really believe that?'

'Does it matter? She chose to wait and come into town with you.'

'She wanted to come on her own.'

'Oh, for heaven's sake, I could shake you!' She took a deep breath, then, slowly, talking to him as if he were a child, she said, 'Don't you understand? Xandra got herself suspended from school deliberately. Mrs Warburton would have let her go and visit her grandfather in hospital, but she didn't want an afternoon off school. She wanted to be with you.'

'That's ridiculous,' he said. He took another step but Annie didn't budge. 'I tried,' he said. 'It's not easy from the other side of the Atlantic, but I've tried and tried to be a father—I even applied for joint custody.'

'The Family Court turned you down?'

'Penny told them that she would be confused. She was already that. Calling her new husband Daddy, ignoring me. Wouldn't come and see me in London when I was here on business. Wouldn't come to the States, even when I offered the theme park incentive.'

'She doesn't want theme parks,' she said. 'She wants you.'

'But—'

'Not in America, not in London, but here.'

He spread his arms, indicating that she'd got what she wanted.

'That's just the beginning. She's not going to make it easy for you. She'll test you and test you. Keep pushing you away to see how resilient you are. Whether you love her enough to stay.'

'She knows I love her,' he protested. 'I've given her everything she's ever wanted. Ever asked for.'

'Except yourself. She wants you, here, in her life. Not some Santa figure with a bottomless cheque book, but a father. She's afraid that you've only come to close down the garage, tidy up the loose ends, and she's desperately afraid that this time when you leave you'll never come back.'

'How can you know that?' he demanded, not wanting to believe it.

'Because I tested everyone. Not with tears or tantrums, I just withheld myself. Made nannies, governesses, teachers, even my grandfather prove that they weren't going to go away and never come back, the way my parents had.'

'I came back.'

'How often? Once a year? Twice?' She put her hands on his shoulders, forced him to look at her. 'How much do you want to be a father?' she demanded. 'Final answer.'

'Enough not to turn a blind eye to hot-wiring cars or making secret plans to meet up with boys.'

'Right answer,' she said, with a smile that made the lights seem dim. 'Come on, let's go and say hello.'

'Hello?' he said, staying put. 'That's it?'

'It's a start.'

'But—'

Annie felt for him. She could see that he wanted to go over there and grab that boy by the throat, demand that he never come near his precious little girl.

'Open your eyes, open your ears, George. Listen to what she's telling you. She wants you to be part of her life but you're going to have to accept that she's a young woman.'

George tore his gaze from his daughter and looked at her advocate. Passionate. Caring.

'You're not talking about her,' he said. 'You're talking about yourself.'

She didn't answer. She didn't have to. It was obvious. When she was six years old her life had changed for ever. At sixteen she'd become a national icon and had never had the freedom to meet a boy in town. Test herself. Make mistakes.

She knew everything. And nothing. But it was the everything that was important.

'Okay,' he said, 'let's go and say hello.'

'And?' she said, still pushing him.

'And what?'

'And ask him if he likes Chinese food,' she said.

He took a deep breath. 'Let's go and say hello. And ask him if he likes Chinese food.'

'You ask him while I get the skates,' she said, straightening, taking a step back. 'What size do you take?'

'Skates?' He groaned. 'Please tell me you're kidding.'

'I've only got a week. Less. I'm not missing out on a single opportunity.'

'Couldn't you just wait until you go home?' he

asked. 'Get your personal assistant to call some Olympic champion to give you a twirl around the ice?'

'I could,' she agreed, 'but I wouldn't be that self-indulgent.' He was being facetious, she knew. He'd briefly let down his guard and now he was using sarcasm to keep her at a distance. No deal. If he wanted her distant, he was going to have to let her go. 'And, anyway, where would the fun be in that?'

'You're saying that you'd rather go out there and be pushed, shoved, fall over, make a fool of yourself in public?'

'Exactly like everyone else,' she said, 'but I don't need you to hold my hand. If you'd rather watch from the sidelines I'd quite understand.'

George growled with frustration.

She was an enigma. A woman of supreme confidence who was at home with the powerful and the most vulnerable. Touchingly innocent and yet old beyond her years. Clear-sighted when it came to other people's problems, but lost in the maze of her own confusion.

On the surface she had everything. She had only to express a wish for it to be granted. Any wish except one. The privacy to be herself.

He regarded her—her eyes were shining with a look of anticipation that he'd seen before—and for a moment he forgot to breathe as he revised the number of impossible items on her wish list to two.

The second should have been tailor-made for a man who had made a life's work of the no-strings-attached, mutually enjoyable sexual encounter. It was the perfect scenario. A beautiful woman who would, in the reverse of the Cinderella story, on the seventeenth of December change back into a princess.

But Annie had, from the first moment she'd turned that penetrating gaze full on him, set about turning his life upside down.

Within twenty-four hours of meeting her he was beginning to forge a shaky relationship with his daughter, was talking to his father and found himself thinking all kinds of impossible things both before and after breakfast.

And accepting one irrefutable truth.

If he made love to Annie, he would never be able to let her go.

But she wasn't Annie Rowland. She was Lady Roseanne Napier and, no matter what her eyes were telling him, they both knew that she could never stay.

'Well?' she demanded impatiently.

'Have you ever been on ice skates?' he asked.

'No, but they're all doing it,' she said, turning to look at the figures moving with varying stages of competence across the ice. 'How hard can it be?'

'They all had someone to hold their hand when they did it for the first time.'

Skating he could do. Holding her hand, knowing that he would have to let go, would be harder, but a few days of being ordinary would be his gift to her. Something for her to look back on with pleasure. For him to remember for ever.

She looked back at him, hesitated.

'What are you waiting for?' he asked. 'Let's go and get those boots. Just don't complain to me when you can't move in the morning.'

'What about Xandra?' she asked. 'That boy?'

He glanced at them, sitting on the bench talking, laughing.

'They can take care of the bags.'

Annie felt the pain a lot sooner than the next morning. She'd spent more time in close contact with the ice than gliding across it—would have spent more but for George—and had been laughing too much to waste time or breath complaining about it.

George was laughing too as he lifted her back onto her feet for the umpteenth time. 'Hold onto my shoulders,' he said as he steadied her, hands on her waist, then grabbed her more tightly as her feet began to slide from beneath her again. Too late. They both went down.

'Have you had enough of this?' he asked, his smile fading as, ignoring the skaters swirling around them, he focused his entire attention on giving her exactly what she wanted. 'Or do you want to give it one more try?'

One more, a hundred times more wouldn't be

enough, Annie knew. She wanted a lifetime of George Saxon's strong arms about her, holding her, supporting her. A lifetime of him laughing at her, with her.

'Aren't we supposed to be shopping for lights?' she said, looking away.

Xandra and her new boyfriend were leaning on the rail watching them. 'Pathetic,' she called out, laughing at the pair of them. 'Give it up.'

'She might have a point,' Annie said, turning back to George.

'She hasn't the first idea,' he said, his expression intent, his lips kissing close. And neither of them were talking about ice skating.

While the skaters whirled around them, in their small space on the ice the world seemed to stand still as they drank in each other. Every moment.

'Come on,' Xandra called. 'Dan knows a great place to buy lights.'

Annie scrambled to her feet and, for the first time since she'd stepped onto the ice, her feet were doing what they were supposed to as she glided gracefully to the edge of the rink with George a heartbeat behind her.

'Dan?' he said.

'Dan Cartwright.' The boy stuck out his hand. 'We met this morning, sir. At the farm.'

'I remember,' George said, taking it.

The boy didn't actually wince but he swallowed hard.

'I'm Annie,' she said, holding out her own hand so that George was forced to relinquish his grip. 'Shall we go and look at these lights?'

The tree lights were just the start. They piled icicle lights for the eaves, curtain lights for the walls, rope lights for the fence into their trolley. And then Annie spotted a life-size reindeer-driven sleigh with Santa himself at the reins and refused to leave without it.

'We won't be able to get it into the car,' George protested.

'Dan's got a motorbike,' Xandra said. 'He's got a spare helmet so I could go home on the back of that.'

'No,' he replied without hesitation. 'You can't.'

'In fact,' she said, carrying on as if he hadn't spoken, 'when I go to Maybridge High I'll need some transport. You had a motorbike, didn't you?'

Yes, he'd had a bike, but that was different. She was a... 'If you want to go to Maybridge High I'll drive you there myself,' he snapped back.

There was a pause, no longer than a heartbeat, while the reality of what he'd said sank in.

He would drive her. Be here. Change his life for her...

'Oh, *please*!' She rolled her eyes. 'How pathetic would I look? Besides, Dan said he'd teach me to ride.'

'I've never been on a motorbike,' Annie cut in

before he could respond. 'Why don't I go with Dan?' Then, 'Actually, I'd love a lesson too.'

'No one is going on the back of Dan's bike!' he exploded. 'And if anyone is going to teach anyone to ride anything, it will be me!'

'Brilliant,' Xandra said, then, just as he realised that he'd been stitched up like a kipper, she nudged him with her shoulder and said, 'Thanks, Dad.'

Dad...

He looked at Annie. She had her hand to her mouth, confirmation that he hadn't misheard, hadn't got it wrong, but something amazing had just happened and he had to swallow twice before he could manage, 'We could come and pick up the sleigh tomorrow in the four-wheel drive.'

'Great. I can get my hair cut at the same time.'

'Whatever you want, Annie,' he replied, and meant it. 'Now, shall we get out of here and pick up some food? Dan? Chinese?'

'Well?' Annie asked, giving a twirl so that George, who'd been waiting for her in a coffee shop opposite the hairdresser, could fully appreciate the stylish elfin cut that now framed her face. 'What do you think?'

'It doesn't matter what I think,' he replied. 'The question is, are you happy?'

'Absolutely,' she said. 'I love it. Even better, no one in there even suggested I looked like...anyone else.'

'A result, then. Although when you reappear in public sporting your new look, they might just wonder.'

'They might wonder, but I've got the pictures to prove I'm in Bab el Sama,' she said, indicating a newspaper left by one of the café's patrons. 'Actually, that's the one downside. Poor Lydia doesn't get a choice in the matter. She's going to have to have her hair cut whether she wants to or not.'

'It goes with the job, but if it worries you buy her a wig for Christmas,' he suggested.

'You're not just a pretty face,' she said, slipping her arm in his. 'Now, let's take a look at this Christmas market.'

'Really? What happened to hating Christmas?'

'Not this Christmas,' she said as they wandered amongst the little stalls decorated with lights and fake snow, admiring the handmade gifts and decorations. 'The new memories I've made will make this a Christmas I will always cherish.'

'That makes two of us,' he said.

They drank gingerbread lattes to warm themselves, tasted tiny samples of every kind of food, bought some of it, then stopped at a stall selling silly seasonal headgear.

'I have to have one of those,' Annie said and George picked up an angel headband which he settled carefully on her head.

'Uh-uh. The angel is on holiday.' She pulled it off

and replaced it with one bearing sprigs of mistletoe that lit up and flashed enticingly. 'Let's give this one a test run,' she teased, closing her eyes and tilting her face to invite a kiss.

His cold lips barely brushed her cheek and, about to pull it off, ask the stallholder if he had something a little more effective, something in George's eyes stopped her. Not the warning to behave that she anticipated, but the mute appeal of a man for whom one more kiss would be one too many. An admission that while he'd walked away from temptation it had not been easy. That he was on a knife-edge.

'Perfect!' she exclaimed brightly as she turned swiftly away to check the rest of the stall. 'This for you, I think,' she said, choosing a Santa hat. She wanted to put it on him, just as he'd put on the angel headband. Pull it down over his ears, cradle his dear face, kiss him so thoroughly that he'd fall.

Yesterday she might have done. Yesterday he'd been this sexy, gorgeous man who'd turned her on, lit her up like the Christmas tree in the square. Today, with one look, she knew that one kiss was never going to be enough. Understood what he'd known instinctively. That walking away after anything more would tear her in two.

So she simply handed him the hat and left him to pay for it, stepping quickly away to look at a stall selling handmade jewellery. Giving them both space to take a breath, put back the smiles, continue as if the world hadn't just shifted on its axis.

She chose a pair of pretty snowman earrings for Xandra, a snowflake brooch for Hetty, a holly tie-tack for George's father and had them put in little gift bags. Just something to thank them for accepting her as she was—no trappings, just ordinary Annie.

She didn't buy anything for George.

She'd already given him her heart.

'All done?' he asked, joining her, and she nodded but, as they were leaving, she spotted the same angels that had been on sale at the Christmas tree farm and stopped. 'I have to have one of those,' she said.

'You're really getting into the Christmas thing,' he said, taking the bag while she paid for the angel.

She shook her head. 'It's for the tree at King's Lacey. A discordant note of simplicity amongst the ornate designer perfection to remind me...' She faltered and, when he didn't press her, she said, 'Let's go home.'

George gave the reindeer a final tug to test the fixing, making sure that it was secure.

'Switch it on,' he called down. 'Let's see if it works.' He was leaving it as long as possible before he was forced to climb down. He felt safer up here on the roof, as far from Annie as he could get.

He'd known a week would be hard, he just hadn't realised how hard. How hard he'd fallen.

He'd never believed in love at first sight and yet from the first moment he'd set eyes on her it had been there, a magnetic pull. Each day, hour, minute he spent in her company was drawing him closer to her. And the nearer he got, the harder it was going to be to break away.

She understood, he knew. Had been careful to keep her distance since that moment at the market when she'd lifted her face for a kiss—he'd kissed her before without invitation, after all—and he hadn't been able to do it. Not kiss her and let her go.

She'd urged him to get involved with the renovation of Xandra's car, build on the new start they'd made—not that he'd needed much encouragement. The moment when she'd called him 'Dad' had been a turning point. There was a long way to go, but he was here for the long haul and he'd spent a lot of time on the phone to Chicago, reorganising his life. But that had still left a lot of time to be together.

Time when she got into trouble trying to cook and needed a taster and he'd stayed to help.

Time around the table when, even when they weren't alone, somehow there was a silent connection, something that grew stronger each day.

Time for quiet moments by the fire when his mother and Xandra were at the hospital. Not saying much. Not touching. Just looking up and seeing her curled up in the chair opposite. Being together.

Perfect moments that had felt like coming home.

'Xandra should do the official switch on,' she called back. 'It was all her idea.'

'This is just a test run. She can do it properly later, when it's dark.'

'Okay...' She put her hand on the switch, then said, 'It gives me great pleasure to light up the Saxon family home this Christmas. God bless it and all who live in it.'

She threw the switch and the lights came on, twinkling faintly in the bright winter sunlight.

'It's going to look fabulous when it gets dark,' Annie said, shading her eyes as she looked up at him. 'You've done an amazing job with Santa. He looks as if he's just touched down on the roof.'

There was no putting it off and he climbed down the scaffold tower. 'I suspect I've broken at least half a dozen town planning laws,' he said. 'It'll be a distraction for passing motorists and in all probability an air traffic hazard. And, as for cheering up my father when he gets home, he'll undoubtedly have a relapse at the prospect of the electricity bill when he sees it.'

'Phooey.'

He looked at her. 'Phooey? What kind of language is that for the daughter of a marquess?'

'Completely inappropriate,' she admitted, looking right back at him, and they both knew that he was reminding her that time was running out.

'Annie Rowland, on the other hand, can say phooey as much as she wants. So... Phooey,' she said, clinging to these final hours. Then, turning back to the house, 'Besides, you won't be able to see it from the road. Well, apart from Santa up there on the roof. And the rest of the lights are energy efficient, so a very merry eco-friendly Christmas to you.'

'I'll bet you don't have one of those on the roof of your stately home,' he said a touch desperately. Reminding himself that she wasn't Annie Rowland, that this was a little fantasy she was living. When the metaphorical clock struck midnight she would turn back into Lady Rose and drive off in a limo with chauffeur and bodyguard in attendance, return to the waiting Viscount and the life she was born to.

'They did have another one in the shop,' she said, turning those stunning blue eyes on him. 'Do you think they'd deliver it to King's Lacey?'

'If you were prepared to pay the carriage, I imagine they'd deliver it to the moon, but what would your grandfather say?'

'I've no idea, but the estate children would love it. In fact, I might see if I can hire a Rudolph the Red-Nosed Reindeer sleigh ride for the Christmas party.'

'You have a party?'

'Of course. It's expected. A party for the local children, with Santa in attendance with presents for everyone. The tenant farmers in for drinks on Christmas Eve and then, on Christmas Day, my grandfather and I sit in state in the dining room for lunch before exchanging perfectly wrapped gifts. The only thing that's missing is conversation because, rather than say the wrong thing, we say nothing at all.'

'I find it hard to imagine you tiptoeing around anyone's feelings. You certainly don't tiptoe around mine.'

'I know.' She smiled at him. 'You can't imagine how relaxing that is.'

'So why do you put up with it year after year?' he demanded, suddenly angry, not with her grandfather but with her for enduring it rather than changing it.

'Duty?' she said. 'And my grandfather is all the family I have.' Then, in a clear attempt to change the subject, 'What about you, George? Are you really going to stay on?'

'You suspect I might be pining for my beach bum existence?'

'That would be George Saxon, the beach bum who designed a series of computer programs that helps to reduce wear and tear on combustion engines?' He waited, knowing that she had something on her mind. 'Who's since designed a dozen applications that have made him so much money he never has to work again?'

'Does Rupert Devenish work for a living?' he asked.

'Rupert runs his estates. Holds directorships in numerous companies. Works for charity. He's not idle.'

'It's no wonder the press are so excited,' he said, wishing he hadn't started this. 'You sound like the perfect match.'

The colour drained from her face but, without missing a beat, she said, 'Don't we?' Then, briskly, 'Okay. The lights are done and we've just got time for that motorcycle lesson you promised me before your father gets home from the hospital.'

'For that we'd need a motorcycle,' he pointed out thankfully. 'I thought perhaps, this year, I might break with tradition and, instead of a bank transfer, I'd let Xandra choose her own present. No prizes for guessing what she'll choose.'

It was meant to distract her and it did.

'It'll be a cheap Christmas, then. The only bike she wants is yours.'

'Mine?'

'The one in the barn?'

George glanced at the stone long-barn, all that remained of the original farm buildings. Over the years it had served as a stable, a depository for tack, garden tools and every item of transportation he'd ever owned since his first trike, then crossed to the door and pushed it open.

'What is it?' she asked as he stared at a familiar tarpaulin.

'Nothing,' he said. 'History. A heap of rust.' But, unable to help himself, he pulled back the tarpaulin to reveal the motorbike he'd bought on his sixteenth birthday.

It wasn't a classic. Nothing like the high-powered one he rode in California, but he'd saved every last penny of money he'd earned or been given for birthdays, Christmas, to buy it and it had represented freedom, independence. He'd ridden it home from Cambridge that first Christmas, high on his new life, full of everything he'd done and seen.

Four weeks later, when it was time to return to his studies, Penny had refused to ride on the back because of the baby and they'd taken the train.

CHAPTER TWELVE

'I DON'T see any rust,' Annie said.

'No.'

The bike had been sitting in the barn for fifteen years and for fifteen years someone had lavished care on it, keeping it polished, oiled, ready to kick-start and go.

There was only one someone who could have done that—his father—and he slammed his fist against the leather saddle, understanding exactly how angry, how *helpless* Annie had felt as she'd lashed out at him.

He wanted to smash something. Roar at the waste of it, the stupidity.

'Why didn't he say? Why didn't he tell me?'

'That he loved you? Missed you?'

Annie reached out for him and, wrapping her arms around him, she held him as he'd held her. And he clung to her because she understood as no one else could. Clung to her, wanting never to let her go.

In the end it was Annie who made the move,

leaning back a little, laying warm lips against his cold cheek for just a moment, before turning to the bike.

'Will it start?' she asked.

He didn't care about the damn bike. He only cared about her but, just as he'd kept his distance in the last few days, protecting himself as much as her, now she was the one wearing an aura of untouchability.

Standing a little straighter, a little taller, even wearing a woolly hat and gloves, he had no doubt he was looking not at Annie Rowland, but Lady Rose.

And still he wanted to crush her to him, kiss her, do what she'd asked of him and make her so entirely his that she could never go back.

And that, he discovered, was the difference between lust and love.

When you loved someone your heart overrode desire.

'There's only one way to find out,' he said, un-hooking a helmet from the wall. He wiped off a layer of dust with his sleeve and handed it to her, unhooked a second one for himself, then pulled the bike off its stand and wheeled it out into the yard.

It felt smaller than he remembered as he slung a leg over the saddle, kicked it into life, but his hands fitted the worn places on the handlebars and the familiar throb of the engine as he sat astride the bike seemed to jump-start something inside him.

Or maybe it was Annie, grinning at him in pure

delight. Somehow the two seemed inextricably connected. Part of each other, part of him. Pulling on the helmet, he grinned back and said, 'Well, what are you waiting for? Let's go for a ride.'

She didn't need a second invitation, but climbed on behind him.

'Hold tight,' he warned and, as he took off, she hung on for dear life, her arms around his waist, her body glued to his.

It was beyond exhilarating. The nearness to everything, the road racing beneath them, the closeness, the trust, their two bodies working as one as they leaned into the bends of the winding country roads. It was as if they were one and when, far too soon, they raced back into the garage forecourt, he seemed to know instinctively the exact moment to ease back, turn, put out his foot as they came to a halt in front of the barn door.

Coming home, exactly as he had done countless times in the past.

For a moment the engine continued to throb, then everything went quiet. It was only then, when she tried to move, dismount, that Annie realised that she was not just breathless, light-headed but apparently boneless.

'Oh,' she said stupidly, clinging to George as he helped her off the bike and her legs buckled beneath her. He removed her helmet as if she were a child. 'Oh, good grief, that was—'

George didn't wait to hear what she thought—he knew. Despite the fact that she was so far out of his reach that she might as well be on Mars, that in a few days she would walk away, taking his heart with her, and he would have to smile and pretend he didn't care. Knowing that each touch, each kiss, would intensify the pain of losing her, he kissed her anyway.

He kissed her not to test her probity, not as a prelude to the kind of intimacy that had overtaken them in the kitchen.

It was a kiss without an agenda, one that would endure in his memory and maybe, on the days when Annie felt alone, in hers. A kiss given with a whole heart.

And that was as new for him as it was for her.

That she responded with all the passion of a woman who knew it would be their last made it all the more heartbreaking. Finally, breathlessly, she broke away.

'No,' she said, backing rapidly away, tears streaming down her face. 'I can't do this to you.' Then she turned and ran into the house.

'Annie!'

George's desperate cry still ringing in her ears, Annie raced up the stairs and by the time he caught up with her she had her cellphone in one hand, calling up the taxi firm while she emptied a drawer. She'd never wear any of the clothes again, but she'd bought them with George and they held precious memories.

She'd crammed a lifetime of ordinary experiences into a few days. She'd laughed more than she had in her entire life. She'd loved more. And been loved by Hetty, Xandra, called 'lass' by George senior, which she recognised as a mark of acceptance. While George…

George had made it his purpose in life to give her what she most wanted—to be ordinary—even while taking the utmost care to keep a physical distance between them.

And then he'd found the bike and, overwhelmed by what that meant, for a precious moment he'd let down his guard. It was then, when he'd kissed her in a way that made her feel like the woman she wanted to be, when tearing herself away from him had been beyond bearing—

'What the hell are you doing?' he demanded, bursting into the room, taking the cellphone from her and breaking the connection.

'Leaving,' she said, taking it from him and hitting Redial, throwing the clothes into her bag. 'Now. I should never have stayed.'

George Saxon had a real life, a family who wanted him and nothing on earth would allow her to inflict even the smallest part of her life on them. Somewhere, deep down, she'd hoped that they would be able to remain friends. That she could, once in a while, call him, talk to him. But, if she'd learned one thing this week, it was that for someone you truly loved you would sacrifice anything, even love itself.

Forget Thursday. She couldn't wait until then. She had to leave now. Tonight. Never look back.

George stood there, watching her fling her clothes into a bag and feeling more helpless than he had in his entire life. He said her name, as if that would somehow keep her from leaving. 'Annie.'

She looked up.

'I love you.'

The hand holding the phone fell to her side. She opened her mouth, took a breath, shook her head. 'You don't know me.'

'I know what makes you laugh,' he said, lifting a hand to her face, wiping his fingers across the tears that were running unchecked down her face. 'I know what makes you cry.'

She didn't deny it, just shivered as he put his arms around her, drew her close, resting his own cheek against her pale hair.

'I know how your skin feels beneath my hands,' he continued, more to himself than to her. 'The taste of your mouth. The way your eyes look when I touch you. I know that you're kind, generous, caring, intuitive, smart.' He looked down at her. 'I know that, no matter what I say, you'll go home. What I'm asking is—will you come back?'

'This isn't a fairy-tale, George. Will you call me a taxi? Please?'

There was a note of desperation in that final please, but she'd given him his answer and there didn't seem a lot to say after that.

His mother and Xandra had gone shopping before going to the hospital to collect his father and he left a note on the kitchen table, explaining that a family emergency had called Annie home.

'How long will it be?' she asked when she followed him downstairs. 'The taxi.'

'There's no taxi. The deal was always that I'd take you home.'

She didn't argue, just surrendered her bag, got into his car. Neither of them said another word until they reached the motorway, when she looked at him.

'What?' he asked.

'No...'

'Spit it out.'

'It's Lydia's car. Could you... Would you find a replacement?' She took a paper bag out of the big shoulder bag she carried everywhere, placed it in the glove compartment. 'There should be enough.'

'Just how much money were you carrying around with you?' he demanded.

'Don't you mean where did I have it all stashed?'

His knuckles whitened as his hands tightened on the steering wheel.

'Will you do it?'

'Don't you have some little man who does that kind of thing for you?' Then, 'Oh, no. My mistake.

You can't ask anyone at home. You wouldn't be allowed out on your own for the rest of your life if your grandfather found out what you did.'

'Red would be good, if you could manage it,' she said, her voice even, controlled. Holding everything in. 'I've left her address with the money.'

'Roadworthy. Red. Is that it?'

'I'd like her to have it before Christmas.'

'Do you want me to put on the Santa hat, climb on her roof and push it down the chimney?' He banged the flat of his hand against the steering wheel. 'I could start hating Christmas all over again.'

Annie could understand why he was angry. There were a thousand things she wanted to say, but nothing that would help either of them.

'If there's any money left, will you give it to some local charity?'

'Anonymously, of course. That's it? All debts paid?'

No. Not by a long shot but there was one thing she could do. 'Would you like me to speak to Mrs Warburton? At Dower House. In case Xandra changes her mind about going back.'

'She won't be returning to boarding school.'

'Her mother might not take the same view,' she pointed out.

'Her mother lost her vote when she switched off her cellphone.'

'Yes, well, I'm sure she'll be happier living with you and her grandparents.'

He shook his head. 'I left home when I was eighteen, Annie. I'm not about to move back in with my parents. What about you?'

'What about me?'

'Are you going to go home and grovel to your grandfather for being a bad girl?' he asked, driven by helpless anger into goading her. 'Beg his forgiveness and promise never to do it again?'

'George—'

'Go on playing the part that he wrote for you when you were six years old?'

'Wrote for me?'

'Isn't that what he did?' He'd read her story on the Net, wanting to know everything about her. 'From the moment you stepped into the limelight. Isn't he the one pushing the wedding bells story?'

She didn't answer.

'I saw that photograph of the two of you together on the day it was first published. Your mouth was smiling, but your eyes… You looked hunted.'

He saw the slip road for a motorway service station and took it. Pulling into the car park, he turned on her. 'You told Xandra that you'd only marry Rupert Devenish if you loved him. Do you?'

'George… Don't do this.'

'Do you?'

'No…' The word was hoarse, barely audible. 'Before I met you…'

'Before you met me—what?'

'I might have been that desperate.'

She was no more than a dark shape against the lights. He couldn't see her face or read her expression and that made it easier. One look from those tender blue eyes and he'd be lost.

'What do you want, Annie?' he asked, fighting the urge to just take her in his arms, tell her that it would be all right, that he would make it so. But he knew that this was something she had to do for herself.

She opened her mouth. Closed it again.

'Don't think about it,' he said a touch desperately, wanting to shake her. 'Just speak. Say the first thing that comes into your head. What do you really want?'

'I want to be the person I would have been if my parents had lived,' she blurted out. Then gave a little gasp, as if she hadn't known what she was going to say. 'A doctor,' she said. 'I was going to be a doctor, like my mother.'

That was it? Something so simple?

'So what stopped you?' he asked.

'It was impossible. You must see that.'

'I see only a woman who had a dream but not the courage to fight for it. A quitter.'

'You don't understand—'

'Oh, I understand.' He understood that if she went back like this, afraid to admit even to herself what she wanted, she'd never break free. She'd forced him to take a look at his life, to straighten it out, and now, because he loved her, he was going to fight for her whether she liked it or not. 'I understand that you were enjoying being the nation's sweetheart a little bit too much to give it up,' he said, twisting the knife, goading her, wanting her to kick out, fight back. 'Being on the front page all the time. Everyone telling you how wonderful you were, how brave…'

Her eyes flared in the lights of a passing car and he knew he'd done it. That if she'd had the room to swing her arm she might have slapped him and he'd have welcomed it, but he didn't let up.

'If you'd wanted to be a doctor, Annie, you'd have been one. I'm not saying it would have been easy, but you're not short of determination. What you wanted was your mother,' he said, 'and being her was the closest you could get.'

'No!' There was the longest pause. 'Yes…' And then, with something that was almost a laugh, 'Instead, I became my father. Good works, duty. Everything by the book.' She looked at him. 'Until he met my mother.'

'She was a bad influence?'

'That depends on your point of view. Without her, he'd have been like my grandfather, like Rupert. But my mother came from another world and she stirred his social conscience. Together they used his money, his contacts, his influence to help change the world.' In the darkness he heard her swallow.

'That's why they were targeted, killed. Because they were the kind of people whose death mattered enough to make headlines.'

She didn't say that her grandfather had blamed her mother for that. She didn't have to. But it explained why he'd kept her so close, so protected. Not just from unnamed threats, but so that she wouldn't meet someone like him. Someone who would take her away, as her mother had taken his son, and, from disliking the man on principle, he found himself pitying him.

But it was Annie who mattered.

'You're not a copy of anyone,' he told her fiercely. 'You encompass the best of both of them. Your father's *noblesse oblige*, your mother's special ability to reach out to those in need, her genuine empathy for people in trouble. You make the front page so often because people reach for it. Your smile lights up their day.'

As it lit up his life.

'But—'

'I've seen you in action. You're not acting. That's all you, straight from the heart, but you have to take charge of your life. Hold onto what's good. Walk away from the rest.'

'You make it sound so easy.'

'Nothing worthwhile is ever easy. I've no doubt you'll meet resistance. The "just leave it to us" response. Like punching marshmallow. It's easy to get sucked in. I'm a designer, so I hire the best in the business to run my company.' He smiled, even though she couldn't see his face. 'The difference between us is that I can fire anyone who doesn't do it the way I want it done.'

'I can't fire my grandfather.'

'No. Family you have for life. You told me to talk to my father—actually, you blackmailed me into it. Now I'm going to return the favour. Talk to him, tell him what you want.'

'Or?'

He shrugged, knowing that he didn't need to say the words.

'You're bluffing again.'

'You want to bet?'

There was the briefest pause before she said, 'No.'

'Good call.'

'Hungry?' he asked.

'Surprisingly, yes,' she said.

'Then here comes another new experience for you. The motorway service station.'

'You're going to keep the garage open to specialise in vintage cars?' Annie asked once they were seated with their trays containing pre-wrapped sandwiches and coffee and, because he'd made his point, he was filling her in on his own plans. 'Will Xandra go for that?'

'I mentioned it when we were working on the

Austin yesterday.' George stirred sugar into his coffee, smiling at the memory of Xandra forgetting herself enough to fling her arms around him. 'She knows it's a good niche market. I'll start looking for a manager, staff, in the New Year.'

'So, if you're not going to live with your parents, where will you live?'

'I'm not going to move. They are. I'll buy the farm—'

'Farm?'

'There are just over five hundred acres still let to tenants. Not quite an estate, no park gates, but it's good arable land. I'm going to build a bungalow in the paddock for my parents, something easy to manage.'

'And you'll live in the house.'

The way she said that made him look up. 'It needs some work and I'll have to find a housekeeper, but that's the plan.'

'What about your business?'

'I'll have to make regular trips to Chicago, but I'll turn the barn into an office. Anything I could do in California, I can do here.'

'Everything in one place. The work-life balance achieved. Your extended family around you.'

'You like the idea?'

Annie sighed. 'I'm deeply envious. I totally fell in love with the farmhouse. But won't you miss your place on the beach?'

'There'll be time for that too. Maybe next time

you want a break you should give me a call. We could catch up on those motorbike lessons.'

She shook her head. 'I'm not going to run away again, George.'

'No?'

She swallowed. 'No. Open, upfront. The trouble is that when you've used publicity you can't just turn it off, expect the media to back off just because it's no longer convenient. I come with a lot of baggage.'

He heard what she said. Something more. It was the sound of a woman taking a tentative step away from the past. Coming towards him.

'You'll just have to keep your top on when we're on the beach then,' he replied casually.

For a moment the world seemed to hold its breath.

Then she replied, 'And keep the curtains drawn when we're inside.'

'Actually, taking photographs through the window would be an invasion of privacy.'

'You think they'd care?' she said, faltering.

'If we were married it wouldn't be a story.'

'I never thought of that.'

And suddenly they were talking about a life. The possibility of a future.

'What about Xandra? You've just got your life together.'

'Nothing worthwhile is ever easy, Annie. I've

fought for everything I've got. Worked hours that would have raised the eyebrows of a Victorian mill owner. Say the word and I'd fight the world for you.'

'I have to learn to fight my own battles, George.'

His only answer was to take a little white box from his pocket.

'I was going to give you this before you left. A conversation starter at the Christmas dinner table. Something to make you smile.' He handed it to her. 'When you're ready to try life on Mars, wear them to some dress-up gala and I'll come and spring you.'

She looked up at him, then opened the box. Nestling in cotton wool were a pair of earrings that matched the mistletoe headband. She removed the studs from her ears and replaced them with the earrings. Clicked the tiny switch to set the lights twinkling.

'Are they working?' she asked.

By way of reply, he leaned forward, took her chin in his hand and kissed her, hard. Then he switched them off.

'That's it,' he said. 'Next time I do that it's for keeps.'

He drove, without haste but sooner, rather than the later he would have wished for, they reached the village of Lacey Parva. Annie directed him to the entrance to her grandfather's estate but as they cleared a bend there were dozens of cars, vans, even a TV truck parked along the side of the road.

'Don't stop,' she said, ducking down as he slowed in the narrow lane and everyone turned to look. 'Drive on,' she muttered, scrabbling in her bag for her cellphone.

She switched it on, scrolled the news channels. Used that word she'd learned.

'What?' he asked.

'Lydia's missing,' she said, desperately checking her texts. Her voicemail. 'The world thinks I've been kidnapped.'

'Have you?'

She shook her head. 'No. She's left a message to say that there's nothing to worry about.'

'I'm glad to hear it. So, is there another way into the estate?'

'A dozen, but they'll have them all staked out. Just keep going. I'll show you where you can drop me off. I'll walk to the house.'

'Drop… You expect me to leave you by the side of the road?'

'It's all going to come out, George. If I can get to the house, the PR team can cobble together some story. There's no need for you to be involved.'

'That's it? One setback and you're going to run for cover?'

'You don't understand—'

'I understand,' he replied, his jaw so rigid that he

thought it might break. Mars? Who did he think he'd been kidding? He was so far out on a limb here that Pluto was out of sight. 'But you don't actually have a say in the matter. I'm taking you home through the front gates,' he said, swinging into a lay-by and turning back in the direction of the house. 'It's not open to negotiation, so if being seen with me is going to be difficult, then buckle up. It's going to be a bumpy ride.'

'Stop!' she demanded. 'Stop right here.'

And that, apparently, was all it took. 'Damn you, Annie,' he said as he brought the car to a halt, eyes front, his hands gripping the steering wheel. 'I thought for a minute that we had something. A future.'

'So did I. So what just happened?' she demanded. She was angry with him?

He risked a glance at her, felt a surge of hope, but this wasn't the time to pussyfoot around, it was time for plain speaking.

'Reality? Life?' he offered. 'I'm an ordinary man, Annie, from ordinary people. Yeoman stock. Farmers. Mechanics. Why would you want a Saxon when you should have a prince?'

'Ordinary,' she repeated. 'It wasn't dukes or barons that made this country great. It was hard-working, purposeful, good people like your family. *Extraordinary*, every one of you.'

She reached out, took his hand from the wheel, held it in hers.

'I love you, George Saxon, and I would be the proudest woman in Britain to be seen on every front page in the world with you, but this is going to be a media feeding frenzy. I simply wanted to protect you, protect your family from the fallout of my pathetic lack of courage. I should have talked to my grandfather years ago. I won't let another night pass without telling him what I want.'

'What do you want, Annie?'

'You. A house filled with little Saxons. Xandra. Your parents. You…'

'You've got me, angel. The rest comes included.' And he lifted the hand holding his, kissed it. 'As for the hounds at the gate, maybe the answer is to give them a bigger story than you disappearing for a week.'

'Oh? What story did you have in mind?'

He smiled. 'Switch those earrings on and I'll show you.'

They could have spent the entire evening parked up in the wood but there were people to call, explanations to be made and they spent the next fifteen minutes making phone calls.

'What did your family say?' Annie asked.

'My mother is thrilled. My father said I don't deserve you. Xandra said, "Cool". Yours?'

'My grandfather is so relieved that I could have announced I was marrying a Martian,' she said.

'Then all we have to do is tell the world. Ready?'

'Ready.'

He kissed her once more, then drove slowly up to the gates of King's Lacey.

Cameramen surged forward as a policeman came to the window.

'Lady Roseanne Napier,' he said. 'George Saxon. We're expected.'

He peered in. 'Lady Rose! You're a sight for sore eyes. We've all been worried sick.'

'Just a misunderstanding, Michael. We'll make a statement for the press and then, hopefully, you can go home.'

'No rush, madam,' he said, opening the door for her, waving the press back. 'The overtime comes in handy at this time of year.'

There was a volley of flashes as she stepped from the car. 'Lady Rose! Who was the man in Bab el Sama, Lady Rose?'

'I'm afraid I've no idea,' she said, holding out a hand as George joined her. 'I haven't left England all week. And this is the only man in my life,' she said, turning to him. Smiling only for him. 'George Saxon. The man I love. The man I'm going to marry.'

For a moment they could have heard a pin drop. Then they lit up the night with their cameras as George lifted her hand to kiss it.

It was a photograph that went around the world.

Daily Chronicle, 10th June

FAMILY WEDDING FOR LADY ROSE

Lady Roseanne Napier was married yesterday to billionaire businessman, Mr George Saxon, in the private chapel on her grandfather's estate at King's Lacey.

Miss Alexandra Saxon, the groom's daughter by an earlier marriage, attended the bride, along with children from her grandfather's estate.

The wedding and reception were a quiet family affair, despite a bidding war from gossip magazines who offered a million pounds to charity for the privilege of covering the affair.

The groom made a counter bid, pledging five million to charity if the media left them in peace to enjoy their special day with their family and friends, something we were happy to do.

This photograph of the couple, released to the press by the happy couple, is copyrighted to Susanne House and that charity will benefit from its publication.

We understand that the couple will honeymoon in the United States.

* * * * *

A CHRISTMAS TRADITION

Some years ago, when I'd taken my Christmas cards to the post and felt slightly sick when I realised just how much money I'd spent mailing greetings to every corner of the world, I made a decision that in the future I would send my greetings via the Internet and give the money saved to charity; a far greener, and much more lasting way of wishing the world a Merry Christmas and Happy New Year.

Since then, Third World communities have benefited from, amongst other things, a camel, a trained midwife and a goat, but cards are a hard habit to give up. There are always some truly special people you want to reach out to. Some very senior aunts. Faraway friends. People who have done something special for you during the year whom you want to thank with a special wish. For those two or three dozen people we make our own cards.

This isn't one of those 'craft' things. We don't sit down with paper and ribbons and glue—no one would thank me for anything I made like that. Instead my husband and I go through the photographs taken on trips throughout the year and pick out some moment we really want to share with friends and family.

A mist-shrouded castle, autumn woods, a favourite beach.

Last year we went to Bruges, and whilst there John took a photograph of Michelangelo's beautiful 'Madonna and Child' in the Church of Our Lady. As we looked through the photographs we'd taken through the year the image leapt out as the perfect subject for our card.

It's not just a question of printing a few cards, though. We spend a lot of time together choosing a card that works best with the image—gloss, silk, matt. Then there's the font style and colour, the words. It's truly a joint effort until that point, but once all the details have been decided I leave it to John to work his magic with the computer. My job is to write the envelopes, stick on the stamps, walk across to the box to post them.

It has, in a very short time, become a special Christmas tradition. One that sits happily alongside the cards I post on my website and blog. And beside the Oxfam catalogue from which I choose my Christmas card to the world.

A joyful Christmas and a peaceful New Year to you all.

Liz

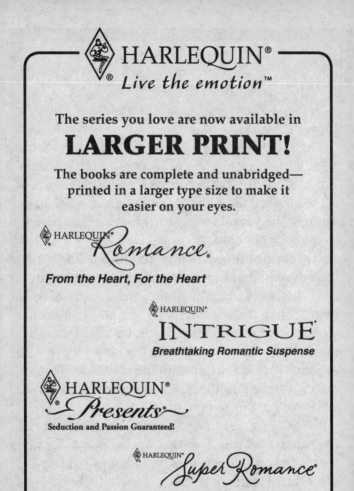

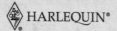

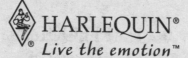

HARLEQUIN®
INTRIGUE®

BREATHTAKING ROMANTIC SUSPENSE

Shared dangers and passions lead to electrifying romance and heart-stopping suspense!

Every month, you'll meet six new heroes who are guaranteed to make your spine tingle and your pulse pound. With them you'll enter into the exciting world of Harlequin Intrigue— where your life is on the line and so is your heart!

THAT'S INTRIGUE— ROMANTIC SUSPENSE AT ITS BEST!

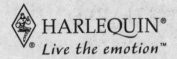

HARLEQUIN®
Live the emotion™

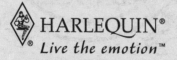

Harlequin® Historical
Historical Romantic Adventure!

*Imagine a time of chivalrous
knights and unconventional ladies,
roguish rakes and impetuous
heiresses, rugged cowboys
and spirited frontierswomen—
these rich and vivid tales will
capture your imagination!*

*Harlequin Historical . . .
they're too good to miss!*

HHDIR06

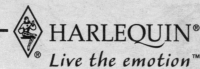